# The Prince of Withy Woods

Cover-design by Cherie Fox

ISBN 9798682842841

For Jamie, Ben, and Imogen,
wishing you success in all your
quests.

# The Prince of Withy Woods

## Book 2 of stories from Seywarde

Vivien Edmundson

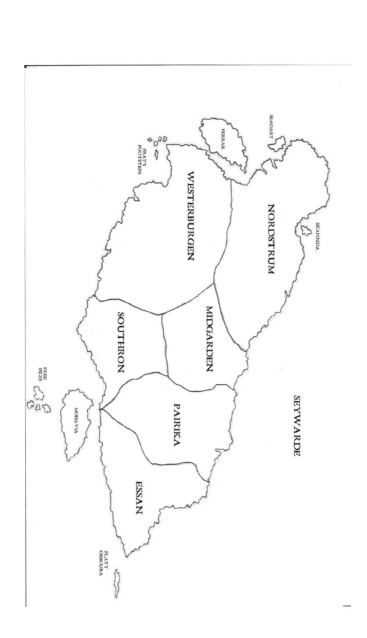

White mountains

Skannda

Wulshaven

Grittas Teeth

Norvik

Galenglass Hills

Seagart

Kenfig

Charlake

Koppelburg

Barrel Tops

Great North Way

Burlap

Horserace Downs

Ferrar

Riversholm

Medenhall

Preceptory of the Plains

Bourpré

Dom Rei

Greenwood

Sanctuary of the Marsh

Withy Woods

Touchstone

Fray's Footsteps

Summerton

Crouchstone Downs

Rushymede

West Meols Road

Shierling Cliff

Piersport

Diamare

Traders Bay

# SEYWARDE

N
E
W
S

...Hills

Kenig

*Wildwater*

*Horteraca Downs*

Preceptory of the Plains

Eyrie

*Silverbolt*

Dom Rei

Touchstone

Shydding Forest

Summerston

Shahanna Desert

Crouchstone Downs

Planitor

Dom d'Or

East Marsh Road

West Marsh Road

Orchards End

Platt Obscura

Fleet

East Road

Diamare

...rt Bay

Mohavia

Free Isles

According to Tusitala, teller of tales, Seywarde is all that remains of an ancient continent, Seaforth.

He says there was a great war between the ice giants, the dragons and the gods, and Seaforth was their battleground. Ice giants froze it, dragons set fire to it, and gods drowned it trying to put out the flames. The continent sank, but traces of it remain; Seywarde and islets round it.

Ice giants continue to lay claim to Seywarde, holding the snow-capped mountains in Nordstrum in their freezing grip. The Shahanna desert in Essan burns as hot as dragonfire. The water gods hold sway in the tumbling rivers of Westerburgen. They guard the remnants of their little kingdoms jealously, so the island is a microcosm of warring climates.

Seywarde is roughly the shape of a squashed egg. It's approximately 220 miles from Wulfshaven in the White Mountains to Dom d'Or in the east, as the crow flies. From Diamare in the south to Kenfig, it's about 100 miles, coast to coast.

The country is divided into six regions: Nordstrum, Westerburgen, Midgarden, Southron, Pairika and Essan. Tusitala says that although Seywarde is a small egg, the inhabitants regard these regions as separate kingdoms, and that this illustrates the arrogance of little islanders.

\*\*\*

# Prologue

Back in the mists of time, the gods had enjoyed a game called Pass the Puck. The way it worked was this: each player chose a country on Seywarde to defend. Then, mounted on the shoulders of an ice giant, he or she would hit the puck into a rival god's patch, using a trident, thunderbolt, uprooted tree, or whatever was his or her weapon of choice. The defending god would try to whack the puck away into another country before it landed. The puck was a gigantic boulder the size and weight of a mountain. It had, in fact, *been* a mountain, before the gods had requisitioned it for their game, and subsequently bashed it about a bit.

The inhabitants of the capital, Dom Rei, signed a strongly-worded petition pointing out that it wasn't much fun watching a rock of megalithic proportions hurtle out of the sky and crush your city. They sent the High Priest, Het Het Hatchu, up Paramount to deliver it to the gods.

Hatchu returned with a nervous tic, swivelling eyes, and the desire to become a hermit. You had to approach his cave very quietly, or he'd scream and curl up in a corner, whimpering. His account of his experiences consisted of incoherent warnings and a lot of 'ohgods, ohgods, ohgods…'

Afterwards the gods had relented and the game hadn't been played in ages. But the chief god, Oculus Optimus Maximus, had been expert at the game, and clung to its spirit, if not its practice.

Oculus had three eyes which saw the Past, Present and Future, all at the same time. It's a talent which would make anybody moody. He was a young god, sometimes lacking in self-confidence. This can happen when your father has eaten all your siblings. Not surprisingly, he sometimes got depressed, and muttered things like 'Why me?' and 'What's it all for?' After a few centuries, he decided he needed a break. So he secretly stopped taking the eyedrops which kept his divine gift in tip-top condition.

He figured he could get away with it for a while. He'd suggest the gods took a holiday. There might be tricky moments if they suspected he wasn't on top of his game, but he was pretty sure he could weasel his way out. You don't get to be chief god without being good at weaseling. He'd shift attention onto something else, or say he had a headache…just for a decade or two, just for a bit of relief from having to be awesome all the time…

He was very good at passing the puck.

\*\*\*

The largest of the countries making up the kingdom of Seywarde was Westerburgen, sometimes called the Wetlands. It was forested, criss-crossed by river valleys, and was quintessentially hunting, shooting, and fishing country.

A cluster of little islands off the coast was called Fray's Footsteps. According to Tusitala, teller of tales, the Water goddess, Aquaphraya, flew down to Seywarde on a seagull's back. She leaped off the gull's back and used the islands as stepping-stones to reach dry land and deliver the Pantheon's message to an astonished fisherman. He built a wooden shrine to commemorate the event. Hundreds of years later, the shrine had become a prosperous temple dedicated to the entire Pantheon of gods and goddesses, and known as The Sanctuary of The Marsh.

Built on a promontory, it was almost a province in its own right, stuck out into the sea and separated from the rest of Westerburgen by the Barrel Tops to the north and Pike Race to the east. Holiday-makers, called pilgrims, came to see the place where Aquaphraya's divine foot had first touched Seywarde. Scholars visited to consult with the head of the Sanctuary, Patroness Hildegarde, as, from time to time, did members of the Witan. Hildegarde liked to keep abreast of current politics.

The precepts Aquaphraya brought to mortals were:

1. Look after other people, especially those less fortunate. This means you must first look after yourself, or you'll be no earthly use to anyone else.

2. Enjoy to the full the life you've been blessed with; to do otherwise would be ungrateful.

3. Hard work never hurt anyone. Overdoing it does. And remember to bend your knees and keep a straight back when you're lifting.

To remind themselves of these rules, the people of Seywarde made the triple sign, touching their thumbs to their foreheads, chins and mouths. Over time, the significance of the sign was forgotten, and it became simply a gesture to ward off evil. And people began to interpret the rules in surprising ways. For example, the gods didn't mention fasting to the point of starvation, straw mattresses, and interrupting a good night's sleep with mumbled prayers in a cold cell. However, these practices were adopted by a cult of young women devoted to Oculus. They called themselves The Little Sisters of Justice, and attracted adherents of a severe and punitive disposition.

The Pantheon did not suggest that getting up early made you morally superior or that staying up late was anybody's business but your own. But the smug Seers of Lorelai, goddess of the Dawn, thought differently. What had begun as a joyous celebration of the dawn became a deadly competition, as the Seers vied to become the earliest riser, and therefore the most devout. Some cheated by not sleeping at all, and either dropped dead from exhaustion, or were found out and expelled. Their obsession may have had something to do with their mapping of the constellations. Or their inherent smugness.

The Seers of Piersport took things further. They questioned people in the street, demanding to know what time they went to bed and at what hour they rose, and pinned up lists naming those whose behaviour did not conform to their own. They rapped on the windows of houses lit at curfew, telling the occupants to get to bed. They returned at sunrise to bang on the doors of those still asleep, accusing them of wasting profitable daylight hours and thus insulting the goddess.

They were so busy interfering with other people's business, they had no time to watch the dawn rise, so had the distinction of being the most unpopular branch of the Order. They annoyed people to the point of violence at the end of pointy knives. Or in the case of vampires, who are sensitive about sleeping arrangements, at the end of pointy teeth.

In contrast, the temples devoted to Volte, the god of Fire, were well-supported and wealthy. Mainly because the Red Fryers scared everyone rigid. They had come up with the interesting concept of the Seven Levels of Hell. They frightened people into giving alms to save them from the everlasting fires of the Netherworld. How many levels you could avoid was calculated on a sliding scale. For a donation of fourpence, the Fryers' prayers ensured you were safe from levels 1 to 3—lukewarm, uncomfortable, pretty damn hot. For an annual price of elevenpence you could avoid all seven, which was a good discount if you could afford that much all in one go.

Patroness Hildegarde was too sensible to make living a decent life more difficult than it already was. But she'd become increasingly disturbed by the bizarre new temples springing up, which she blamed on the gods' off-hand attitude to Seywarde. As head of the Sanctuary, Hildegarde had a hotline to the Pantheon. She knelt and tuned in every day, keeping her back straight, to voice her concerns to the gods.

***

4

The letter arrived at Old Hall at midday. Blaise could remember the time precisely, because he'd never had a letter before. His substantial weight was perched on a stool, and he was watching the spit on which pieces of pork were roasting. As usual, his face was red and he was perspiring. The skin on the meat had turned crisp and brown. Fat had stopped dripping into the pan underneath. The meat was done to a turn of the spit.

'Are you sure? For Blaise?' said Priss, the new scullery maid.

'Wouldn't be much good at my job if I couldn't read, sweetheart,' said the messenger. 'You learned to read since I were here last?'

Priss had slammed the door in his face. She took her ill-temper out on Blaise by throwing the letter into the ash at his feet.

'Can't think why anyone would write to *you*, Blaise!'

And then, when he'd just smiled, she'd felt ashamed, and busied herself with the vegetables.

Blaise had wiped the ash from the thick cream paper. He could read, because Mistress Jessup had taught him his letters, and he recognised his name. He had time to see the paper was folded in three, a blob of red wax securing it. Then he felt the flick of a tea-towel and Mistress Jessup leaned over his shoulder and said, 'That pork burns and I'll give you such a tanning, Blaise, big as you are!' So he'd slipped the unopened letter inside his shirt.

Mistress Jessup had the kitchen range blasting out heat even on a hot day. At curfew Blaise would bank the coals down, but woe betide him if the housekeeper didn't have the beginnings of a decent cooking fire in the morning. So he slept under the table. It was late before he had the kitchen to himself. He wiped his hands on his shirt, drew out the letter, and broke the seal. By the glowing embers he read:

*Hepworth and Tremble*
*Lawyers and Agents*
*17 Outlane*
*Touchstone*

*Blaise Pilgrim,*
   *Pleased be advised that should you contact us at the aforementioned address, we may have information to your advantage.*
   *That is to say that we, the aforementioned Hepworth and Tremble, do not affirm that such information* **will** *be to your advantage. It will be offered* at your own risk. *That is to say, the risk of the addressee.*
*Yours etc.*
*Hieronymus Hepworth (for Hepworth and Tremble).*

A week later, Blaise barrelled down the road to Touchstone, the letter inside his shirt under his jerkin. Mistress Jessup had sent him to the market for some kitchen stores. He found the stalls he needed as quickly as possible so that he would have time for his own errand. He was making his way from the market when he came face to face with Solly Potts.

'Eh up! By 'eck, Porky, you're sweatin' like a bull! There's a trail of lard all the way from Old Hall!'

Solly had spoken deliberately loudly so that the people nearby could hear him. He only came up to Blaise's chin, but he was a handsome boy and enjoyed being the centre of attention.

'Looks like the cook will be roastin' *you* 'afore long!' Solly poked Blaise's stomach. One or two children giggled.

'Leave off, Solly,' said Blaise, amiably.

'Oh, la-di-dah!' said Solly. He grinned at the children. 'He ain't got time for us ordinary folk, livin' up at the Hall! And what exactly is it you do there, Porky, that makes you better'n us? 'Cos I thought you was nothin' but a turnspit!'

Some customers turned round at his raised voice. He gave Blaise another poke in the ribs. Blaise feared the horseplay would dislodge his letter, and brushed away Solly's hand with a tolerant smile.

'Let me be, there's a good fellow.'

Solly hadn't got the rise out of Blaise he wanted, and people were frowning at him and moving away. His grin turned to a frustrated scowl. 'I don't take orders from a kitchen boy!' He launched himself at Blaise, butting him in the stomach.

Blaise, taken by surprise, gasped and toppled over onto his back. Then Solly was on top of him, pummelling him with his fists. At first Blaise tried to grab hold of his arms to stop the beating, but Solly was too fast and caught his cheekbone and nose with a swingeing blow that brought tears to his eyes. He thought of the letter, and how this opportunity to visit the lawyers was slipping away, and he became angry. He balled his right hand into a fist, and shouting 'No!' he drove it at Solly's chin. The blow connected and sent Solly flying.

Blaise got up shakily and looked down at Solly. He was lying unconscious in the dust. Stall-holders and shoppers stared. For the first time they saw Blaise as a strapping lad who it might be best not to annoy. Blaise had surprised himself as well, but before he could be delayed further, he quickly turned onto the road to Outlane.

Half an hour later, clutching a basket containing cheese muslin, oats, candles, and a tin of black molasses, Blaise was standing outside a narrow brick building. An inconspicuous brass plate on the wall beside the door read 'Hepworth and Tremble, Lawyers and Agents'. It was so inconspicuous that Blaise walked past it twice before registering it. He wiped his hands on his britches and tugged on the bellpull.

\*\*\*

In their careless adolescence, insofar as immortals have one, the gods had spent aeons walking Seywarde, talking to mortals trying to work out what made them tick. It left them baffled.

They had experimented by casually rewarding some, as you might give a biscuit to an enthusiastic puppy who had learned to sit up and beg. And when they were in the grip of youthful angst (even gods have bad-hair days) they had casually wreaked havoc by turning pretty girls and boys into flowers and trees, or imposing ridiculous tasks on musclebound young men. Mortals felt the gods were having some kind of elaborate joke at their expense, and were left equally baffled.

They thought the gods' fondness for disguise was puzzling, if not downright sneaky. Oculus delighted in fancy dress, and for obscure, presumably ineffable reasons, sometimes appeared in the guise of a bull, swan, eagle, or shower of golden coins. None of this was appreciated when startled young ladies suddenly discovered they were the mothers of demigods.

The Pantheon's amorous affections for mortals were fickle. Those of Umbra, goddess of the Night, waxed and waned with the moon. These short-lived affairs led to foundlings being left in caves or on doorsteps. Kindly foster parents, having raised the babe in the bosom of their family, felt ill-used when the child turned out to have superhuman powers and divine good looks, and they could no longer pass off little Helen or Herc as one of their own.

They thought it was unreasonable of the gods to appear as vile-smelling beggars and expect their innate divinity to be recognised. It was equally unfair to take offence if you happened on them in their undisguised beauty. For instance, you don't expect to find the goddess Lorelai having a bath, al fresco, when you're out walking the dogs, so it's a bit much when she has a massive hissy fit.

All in all, mortals felt they had a lot to put up with. They thought the gods took advantage of them. They became wary and resentful. There was a distinct lack of enthusiasm when one of the Pantheon showed up.

The gods sulked, as adolescents sometimes do when they feel misunderstood. So they decided to take a holiday.

They caused a palace to be erected on a dizzily high peak called Paramount. According to the Bewildered Monks of Minch, Paramount was due north the White Mountains and then on till morning. It was east of Platt Obscura. It could be found somewhere to the west, beyond the cold mists of Seagart. Or it was south, a week's sail from the Free Isles. It was in one of those places, or else somewhere entirely different, depending on which of the Bewildered Monks you listened to. They were probably *all* right. Paramount could have been in all of those places *at the same time*. Gods can do that sort of thing.

The palace on Paramount was a sugary-pink confection, with slender towers piercing the azure sky. It had balconies on the upper levels, and tiers of alcoves set into its walls, containing silver statues. Every window and door had delicate columns encrusted with flowers. It looked like a wedding cake with an icing overload. It was currently this shape, because the gods had given in after Lorelai had gone off in an almighty strop.

There had been heated exchanges about the look of the holiday retreat, because the gods couldn't agree. When people go on holiday together, living at close-quarters can make them short tempered. The Pantheon was no different.

Volte, the god of Fire, as dark as the furnaces he loved, insisted the palace had a forge. The sombre Earth goddess, Sessile, favoured something built on ecological lines. With a greenhouse. Bretth, the mercurial god of the Winds, (who was breezily chatty, but whose name, ironically, had a silent 'h') said her idea of a log cabin with a mossy floor sounded more like a dungeon than a holiday home. His own suggestion of a many-windowed edifice open to the gentle zephyrs was rejected on account of the draughts. Umbra, goddess of the Night, said she wouldn't get a wink of sleep unless her rooms were soundproofed against Volte's hammer and Bretth's improvisations on the air-guitar.

But the gods' reaction to Lorelai's suggestion for the palace had been especially cutting, because they'd just laughed. To her mind, in an insultingly indulgent way. Umbra said it sounded like a cheap copy of the fabled castle in Wychwood, where a princess lay in an enchanted sleep. Bretth said her idea would be 'an excrescence on the much-loved carbuncle of Paramount'.

Ridicule is a hard thing for a god to swallow, and Lorelai, the radiant goddess of the Dawn, had taken it badly. Her celestial eyes had clouded. She had tossed her golden curls, always a bad sign, and said none of them took anything she said seriously because she was blonde.

'It's high time I took a stand on behalf of blondes. Anyone who says 'I've had a blonde moment' in that ha-ha-silly-me voice should be struck down and eviscerated! No-one appreciates the complex calculations it takes to bring up a rosy dawn every morning. I've a good mind to take a *real* holiday, and then the world will be plunged into everlasting night, and serve you right for disrespecting me. There's nothing wrong with wanting something pretty!'

And she'd stalked off in an angry froufrou of diaphanous pink gauze, leaving the floor littered with spangles and rose petals.

The gods had capitulated. They didn't want the world to be plunged into darkness, even Umbra. When would she get her beauty sleep if she had to be on duty all the time? And whatever the palace looked like on the *outside* wasn't as important as making sure their individual apartments were constructed to each god's ineffable design. With a carefully neutral Thrones Room (in the *plural*, and in magnolia) in which they could meet without any of them taking offence. Gods are very good at taking offence.

So Oculus Optimus Maximus, the Three-Eyed god, went crown in hand to Lorelai and soft-soaped her back into good humour, and the pink palace came into existence. Oculus continued to soft-soap her, feeling guilty because he had a preference for brunettes, his wife Umbra having the most glorious halo of blue-black hair. But Umbra noticed that her husband was paying court to Lorelai, and got the wrong end of the stick.

It was really tricky being in charge of so many sensitive and jealous divinities. Three eyes was barely enough for the job, even when they were in tip-top condition. And at this point, they weren't.

The Pantheon's palace had many towers, one of which was the Tower of Mystery. At its very top, under a steep roof which rose to a point, was a long-forgotten room resembling Rapunzel's lofty prison. Or a witch's hat. It was occupied by an entity who had many titles, but preferred to be called Cassie Chance, which she thought was more user friendly than the other names.

She seldom had visitors. The spiral staircase to

her room would shift direction and lead to a brick wall, or disappear underfoot and pitch you into an abyss. And the pointy roof of the chamber attracted peculiar magnetic fields which subjected every creature in the vicinity to sudden changes of shape, which was disconcerting for guests. So Dame Chance spent most of her time alone, except for her collection of crystal balls, dice, divination cards, and board games. And Grimalkin. Who was most often a cat, but sometimes, to his annoyance, turned into a lizard, depending on the atmospheric conditions.

On the floor below, only slightly less forgotten, was the Chamber of Marvels. More accurately, the junk room. It was something like your attic or garage, filled with stuff you have no use for at the moment. *At the moment* being the crucial proviso. The truth being you can't bear to throw the things out, so you convince yourself there are good reasons for keeping them. The gods had a similar attachment to items languishing in the Chamber.

Since they were on holiday, the gods had dumped a lot of baggage there. Chariot wheels were piled in one corner. There were padded jupons, and armour of leather, mail, and plate. There were horns of silver, ivory, plenty...and horn. A stack of weapons included swords, flame-throwers, axes, quivers of silver arrows, spears, and a crate of lightning bolts.

There were chests containing talismans and anks,

golden apples, poisoned apples, flying carpets, winged sandals and seven-league boots. In a dusty cardboard box lay three drinking vessels, each with a jewel set into the bowl: a rummer with a ruby, a tumbler with a topaz, and a pot with a pearl. The gods knew one of the gems was poisoned, but had forgotten which, so all were banished to the attic.

An iron-bound box contained talking mirrors, lamps imprisoning sprites, rings of power, wands of rowan, and shields which gave impregnable protection. The box was chained, and had nine locks, because magical items are tricksy and try to escape into temperamental hands—like those of ambitious wizards, vain queens, hole-dwellers and Maxx the Merciless. There were even some cloaks of invisibility, although they didn't take up as much room as the other stuff.

Amongst this jumble were the Sounding-Board and the Scrying-Glass, which the gods had used to keep their ears and eyes on Seywarde. And one day, the gods of Fire and Wind, rummaging in the chamber looking for a board game, uncovered the Scrying-Glass.

Bretth blew off the dust. It was years since they'd used the glass, because furnishing a holiday home takes an eternity. On the screen, all of Seywarde, together with its islands, was laid out before them: a microcosm of different climates, with snowy mountains, river valleys, fertile plains, dry deserts and thick forests…

'There's bacon grease on it,' said Volte irritably. He stabbed a finger at one of the forests. 'You've smudged it. It's gone all foggy.'

Bretth put down his BLT and breathed on the screen.

'Nothing wrong with the glass,' he said. 'I'll bet that's Umbra. She's covered the forest in mist.'

'She shouldn't be doin' that, should she? What's the point of a scryin'-glass if she hides the place?'

'It's cloud cover for her pets.'

'I don't care. Oculus ought to do somethin' about it.'

*** 

Sessile brushed stardust off the Sounding-Board and tuned in. She'd stumbled across it when she'd been looking for some curiously-shaped beans she wanted to try out in the greenhouse. She enjoyed listening in. It was like old times, hearing the buzz of voices rising from Seywarde, more soothing than listening to the Pantheon's quarrels.

'So this is where you've been hiding!'

The goddess of Water pattered through the door and sank down next to her sister, her skirts lapping about her feet. Aquaphraya was restless. Holidays were a bore. She didn't like being stuck in one place. She began painting her toenails blue.

The gentle drone from the Sounding-Board was pierced by a female voice which addressed the

Pantheon at some length.

'What is she saying?' said Aquaphraya. She looked critically at a perfect foot.

Sessile yawned. 'It's always the same thing. She's a serial caller. She's complaining about new cults and temple practices, and why aren't we doing something about it.'

'Why *aren't* we doing something about it?'

'Because we're on holiday. And Oculus doesn't like us to dabble.'

The penetrating voice from the Board sounded cross. Aquaphraya looked up.

'That's little Hildy, bless her! How long has she been sounding off?'

'Since coffee time. Maybe longer. I sometimes nod off.'

Aquaphraya paused, her brush hovering over a toe. 'I don't mean today. A *serial* caller? For how long?'

'Oh, in mortal time? About fifty years. Maybe sixty. Give or take.'

'Sixty years? The poor girl has been calling us for sixty years? And we've never called back?'

'Don't be hasty, Fraya. Oculus doesn't like us having favourites.'

'Since when?'

'Oculus says he doesn't like us interfering.'

'Good Us, Sessie! Interfering is what we *do*.'

And in the Thrones' Room, Oculus, the Three-Eyed god, was being nagged by his wife.

17

'...It's ridiculous!' said Umbra. 'Lorelai only has to shake her curls at you, and you go ga-ga. They're all sniggering behind your back. Did you know?'

Oculus prevaricated. He lied through his divine, perfectly even, white teeth. 'See these eyes? Present, Past and Future? Nothing-hid-from-The-All-Seeing, and the rest of it?'

Umbra's eyes brimmed like drowned stars. Otherwise she'd have seen Oculus had his fingers crossed. He wasn't as perceptive without the eyedrops, and keeping up the deception was proving trickier than he'd thought. And it wasn't working out particularly well for his relationship with his wife.

Umbra bowed her head. Long hair as soft as midnight (and incidentally, as straight as a poker) fell over her pale cheeks. She shed angry tears.

*And on Seywarde, the night sky was wracked by a sudden autumn rainstorm.*

'The thing is, Moon of My Delight, I thought you were too preoccupied to notice,' said Oculus.

'What do you mean?'

But the subject of their argument interrupted. Lorelai, the rosy-fingered goddess of the Dawn, glided to the foot of the dais on which Oculus sat enthroned, and her fluttering gown sent rainbows of light onto the magnolia walls. She smiled up at Oculus and tossed her golden ringlets.

Umbra looked accusingly at her husband, and fled from the room.

'Brilliant timing!' said Oculus.

'You should know,' said Lorelai. 'Or has Umbra clouded your mind, along with everything else?'

Oculus looked shifty.

'Don't tell me! You haven't had that 'little talk' with her you promised, have you?'

'I was on the point,' said Oculus.

'You haven't been on the point for ages. You let Umbra do as she likes. She's wrapped you round her little finger. You're supposed to be the All-Seeing, but you've got a blind spot...'

'If only,' said the Three-Eyed god. He gave a long, gusty sigh.

*On Seywarde, the resulting gale bent trees. Smoke billowed down chimneys, and draughts lifted carpets.*

And in Dom Rei, Alec Dainty was creeping along the landing to the king's bedchamber, dagger drawn, when a wind from nowhere blew out his candle. He lost his footing and pitched headlong down the stairs. They found him next morning pierced by his own poniard. Because despite the 'hands-off' approach to the human race which Oculus had adopted, what goes on Up, also goes on Down.

\*\*\*

The City Guards had been dispatched to break up a fight between two of the new temples. The Temple of the Amalgamated Union of Thurible-Dusters and Pew-Openers, a silent order, was holding a fair. Unfortunately, this coincided with the flag day of the Temple of the Crutched Friars and Wire-Walkers.

The Crutched Friars were skilled aerialists, practitioners of the arts of the trapeze and stilt-walking. They believed the higher they were, the closer they came to the gods. Their leaders, the Sky Spinners, never set foot on the ground, living a precarious life balanced on a high wire. They hooked up buckets of food by means of fishing rods, and lowered the buckets afterwards. When the food had been digested. That morning the friars were out in force, swinging along on stilts, a collection-tin in one hand and a bell in the other.

What began as a starchy argument, conducted in dumb show by the Pew-Openers and Thurible Dusters, about who had first dibs on extracting money from the good burghers of Diamare, had descended into a slanging match. One of the Crutched Friars, teetering on his stilts, had sneered 'Look! No hands!' at a furious Duster and made a gesture suggesting he tried pivoting on his own thurible. The Duster had broken his vow of silence by saying something rude.

And then the rival institutions were at each other's throats. It had taken the guards two hours to part them and march them, bruised and bloodied, back to their temples.

When Mopper came into the mess, she was hot and exasperated. She collapsed onto a bench and ran a hand through her damp curls. It was late autumn, and she and her friends had been working as Guards for eighteen months. She automatically rubbed her left leg. It was lunchtime, and there were only two other guards in the mess, playing cards. The older of the two, a hulking, grizzled man, was on a winning streak. Finally, his companion swore, and her chair scraped on the flags as she pushed away from the table in disgust.

'You've dam' near cleaned me out! I'm off to eat while I've still got a few pence left.'

She strode away, while Dogpole shrugged and pocketed his winnings. He lounged over to Mopper and lit a cigarette.

'Where's Vallora?' she said.

'In The Carter's Arms, I expect.'

Mopper massaged her knee, and sighed.

'Why don't you see the surgeon if it's botherin' you?' said Dogpole.

'It's fine. I'm fed up with street patrol, that's all. It's Rodney. He's always trying to impress me. Yesterday it was how many minutes he can hold his breath under water. Today it's how many bench press sit-ups he can do. Five hours I've been sloggin' round with him. And then two of the temples kicked off. Why can't I be partnered with you?'

'Deputy Staple don't like us. Roddy Blench likes *you*, though.'

Mopper snorted.

'Must be nice havin' an admirer,' said Dogpole. He grinned wolfishly. 'None of 'em likes me.'

'You cheat at cards, that's why. I saw you palm the king.'

'It's the only way to make this job interestin'.'

'See! *You're* fed up, too. We're *all* fed up.'

They strolled off in the sunshine to The Carter's Arms. The benches at the long table were crammed with city workers, who barely had enough elbow room to wield their forks. The landlord and Buckie hurried about carrying platters of stew. It was a noisy place at lunchtime. If you wanted to eat with more privacy, you sat at a table in one of the recesses either side of the hearth. It was a warm day so the towering arrangement of logs was unlit.

They found Vallora sitting in an alcove playing a board game with a prosperous-looking young man.

'Hello,' said Vallora. 'I'm playing draughts.'

'So you are.' Mopper raised a quizzical eyebrow.

Dogpole narrowed his eyes. 'Who the hell is he?'

The stranger looked up. 'Hi. I'm Anders Hjolt.' As there was no response, he said, 'From the Games shop on Parminter Row? Vallora sometimes takes part in our weekend events.'

Mopper goggled at him.

'I don't care what she does in her time off,' said Dogpole, 'but we got to talk to her. Right now. In private.'

'Oh. Well, I guess I'd…I'll be getting back to the shop. See you later, Vallora.'

'I wouldn't count on it, pal.' Dogpole waited until the young man retreated before going up to the counter to order food.

Vallora was staring with fierce concentration into a tankard of ale. Feeling Mopper's eyes on her, she looked up through a curtain of black hair.

'*What*? I can't have a drink at lunchtime?'

'When did you start? Breakfast?'

'So?'

'So I'm the one who's had to cover for you while you played games. Much thanks I'm getting. That's a whole morning listening to Rodney Blench—'

'I think Roddy likes you,' said Vallora.

'Don't change the subject.'

Dogpole joined them, carrying a tray with plates of steaming fish and vegetables, and a loaf cut into buttered slices as thick as doorsteps. Buckie came across to slap three tankards onto the table. Mopper smiled and thanked him and he blushed. Dogpole drank deeply. Vallora took a sip and then pushed the tankard away.

'Thanks, but I've gone off the taste, to be honest.' She helped herself to fish. 'The thing is…well, the Guards…nothing interesting to do, and too much time for thinking. And drinking. An' when you start

23

thinking...an' drinking...Who's that waving at you, Kat? Is it Rodney? He can't keep away.'

They looked through the sooty window. A figure was waving his arms and grimacing at them. They recognised him. It wasn't Officer Blench.

'What's he doin'?' said Dogpole.

He took a pull at his drink. Vallora helped herself to more stew. They regarded the man for a few moments in silence.

'Is he dancin', d'you reckon?' said Mopper.

'Could be, could be. Or else there's midges,' said Dogpole.

They took a considering drink. Vallora chewed slowly and said, 'Shall we call him in?'

'Hang on a bit. I want to see what he does next,' said Mopper. She picked up a spoon and dipped it into her platter.

The skinny man stopped dancing and glared at them, hands on hips. Then he made a gesture.

'Dear me.' Mopper spooned up some onions and gravy.

'Looks like he wants us to meet him outside,' said Vallora.

'You think?'

Dogpole scowled. 'I've only just sat down.'

He filled his mouth with stew, and crooked his finger. The man outside shook his head and hopped from foot to foot, looking anguished. Dogpole shrugged. He pulled off a chunk of bread and sopped up some gravy.

'We should probably investigate what is agitating that honest citizen,' said Vallora.

Mopper snorted.

'Or we could ignore him and go back to the Guardhouse.'

'That sounds like fun,' said Mopper.

'Right then.' Vallora stood up.

Dogpole groaned.

'Come on, Dogpole. Drink up. Let's go and see what Tripp wants.'

***

Their adventures at Old Hall had left Dogpole with a few more scars. His clipped, military-style haircut had grown out, leaving him with shaggy, shoulder-length hair.

Exercise and an outdoor life had toned Mopper's youthful figure. Her left knee, injured in a scrap at the tower, ached in damp weather.

Vallora's sleeves hid the scars of burns on her right arm, another legacy of the fight at Old Hall. She often wore her long hair in the plait favoured by Mohavians. The island was famed for its skilled mariners, but she was not one of them. She'd confessed to her friends that the sea made her ill.

When they left the Merchant Watch, they had little difficulty in being recruited to Diamare's City Guard. They had a letter of recommendation from Captain Bell of Dom Rei. But they were not popular with Captain Fletcher because they had an independent attitude to orders. The Guards were, in their eyes, ill-run and ineffectual. Vallora thought some of them took backhanders to look the other way. And they were all ground down by the daily pettiness of guard duty.

They were following an old acquaintance: thief, entrepreneur and sometime hero, Raphael Tripp. Dogpole collared him in an alley off Cooper Street.

'That's far enough. You've dragged us halfway to the docks. Why in the gods' names couldn't you come inside and talk to us over a drink?'

'Fraternise with the Guard? What would that do to my image?' said Rafi.

It wasn't obvious how having a drink with them would affect his appearance. They hadn't seen him in a while, but he still looked like a ferret down on its luck.

'Well, Tripp, it must be something important for you to risk being seen with us,' said Vallora.

'I knew *you'd* understand.' He looked about and dropped his voice. 'The fact is, I've been at Old Hall visiting Em, and the whole place is in an upset...'

'Nothin' new there,' muttered Dogpole.

'It's not only the mess with the building work.' Rafi paused for effect. 'Blaise has gone missing!'

Mopper looked blank. 'Blaise?'

'Is that the dog?' said Dogpole.

'No, Blaise! You know! The kitchen boy.'

'Oh, yes,' said Vallora. 'I remember. Handy with

a spit hook.'

'Fat lad with a red face?' said Mopper.

'Yes. He's disappeared. Went to Touchstone and ...pouf!'

'He exploded?'

'Muckin' about with gunpowder, was he?' said Dogpole.

'They don't allow gunpowder in The Paradise anymore. Not officially,' said Rafi. 'Not since I was a kid and the Magic Shop blew up. But it's a funny thing, I saw—' He stopped. 'You know I don't mean Blaise exploded!'

They were making fun of him. Emerin had trusted him with an urgent message and he was making a poor job of delivering it. Letting her down was unthinkable. He was flustered seeing them again, and worried that one of the criminal brotherhood from The Paradise might spot him talking to officers. And then there was Vallora, smiling down at him like some goddess amused at the flounderings of a mortal...

'Tell you what, Tripp, why don't we go along to Peat Street,' said the goddess. 'No-one knows you there. And you can start from the beginning.'

In Dogpole's cell-like room, Rafi told them what he knew about Blaise. They'd been thrown together while Rafi had been with Vallora and her friends at Old Hall. Rafi was only a few years older than Blaise, but he was a street-smart kid from The Stews, while Blaise was a naive lad who lived in a

27

rural backwater. Old Hall was his home, and though they teased him, the people there were fond of him. The new staff Lady Melissande now employed, like Priss, might not appreciate him, but everyone else remembered how he'd run out to help when Old Hall was attacked. Emerin was sure Blaise wouldn't simply run away, and that was why she was so worried when he hadn't returned.

Because Rafi was an unthreatening presence and looked like a waif needing to be fed, people talked to him. So Priss had told him about the messenger who'd brought Blaise a letter. Debs, between sobs, said she'd seen Blaise leave for Touchstone a week later, on the morning he'd gone missing. She'd waved from the kitchen door when he'd set off down the drive, so she knew he hadn't taken the cart.

Mistress Jessup listed in detail every purchase she'd instructed Blaise to make. Rafi had listened patiently and then asked about the letter. And yes, she *had* caught a glimpse of it. She remembered she'd been cross with Blaise, the gods forgive her, because he'd been looking at the letter instead of watching the meat. She blamed herself for being sharp with him. When pushed further, she recalled it had a red seal stamped with a set of kitchen scales, like the ones she was currently using to weigh out flour for shortcake. Shortcake was his favourite, she said, and then had to sit down for a good cry.

'You're very good at this, Tripp.' Vallora was struck, not for the first time, by his ability to nose out information.

Rafi blushed. He said that Emerin was upset, so he'd naturally paid attention to what everyone said. And she had told Rafi to remind them that Blaise had helped fight off the men who'd set fire to the tower.

'Em told me to find you, as she was sure you'd want to mount a search for him at once.'

'She told you that, did she?' said Dogpole, drily.

'We'll let you know if we hear anything,' said Mopper, 'but I doubt if Captain Fletcher will be interested in a missing kitchen boy.'

'Captain Fletcher!' Dogpole spat out the words. 'Fletcher ain't interested in anythin' but a soft billet and a bung under the table!'

'You're right,' said Vallora. 'He won't lift a finger. You only get protection when you pay for it. Last week I saw two officers take money from Fiddie the Pick to look the other way. Right outside the Guardhouse, if you can believe it, in broad daylight! He's got a crib sheet as long as your arm. And when I challenged them…'

Mopper opened one of the shutters and stared out of the window. When Vallora was on one of her rants, it was best to give her a few minutes to let off steam. Outside, the sun beat down on Peat Street. There weren't many people around. Most of them would be at work, or having lunch. Her eyes

29

fell on a man standing across the road who was neither at work nor looking for lunch...

'...so I agree with you both,' Vallora was saying. 'Absolutely. Never let it be said that I don't listen to other people's opinions. Rest assured, Tripp, we'll do our best to find that brave boy!'

'Hang on,' said Dogpole, 'I never said...'

'What?' Mopper's attention was wrenched back into the room. 'What have I missed?'

'Thank you.' Rafi gave Vallora his crooked smile for the first time. 'That's a relief. I wasn't looking forward to...well, of *course* it's good to see you again, but I thought you'd be too lofty these days to remember old friends.'

Mopper gave Rafi a sceptical look. He knew Vallora would be stung by a suggestion like that.

'He's a good sort, Blaise,' said Rafi. 'I wouldn't want anything bad to happen to him. I'll shuffle off now, if it's all the same to you.' He left, confident that he'd fulfilled his mission.

Mopper wondered how they'd somehow taken on the search for Blaise themselves. Dogpole shrugged. He'd no objection to a few days away from Fletcher's scrutiny. Vallora was thinking she might have grabbed at Rafi's request for help simply to relieve the mind-numbing boredom of street patrol. But it was more than that. She wanted to be involved in something honest. The casual corruption of the Guardhouse made her skin crawl.

\*\*\*

Deputy Mavely Staple was a balding little man, with a dripping, bulbous nose, and a permanent sniff. He sniffed long and hard when he came across Vallora, Dogpole and Mopper, who he still insisted on calling 'our new recruits', in an attempt to keep them in their places.

He knew he'd reached as high as he could go up the greasy pole. In fact, due to the apathy of the City Guards, Staple had been promoted beyond his capabilities, so he was always on the lookout for the person who'd topple him. He was particularly wary of 'the new recruits', any one of whom could have easily replaced him.

Although he occupied the first point of call for worried citizens—the front desk—his main job was to prevent any effort being required of Captain Fletcher. He'd say that the complaint came under the aegis of the Merchant Watch, or advise them to consult a lawyer. Or he'd require them to fill in pages of complicated forms written in the jargon exclusive to officials. Sometimes Staple even hinted that the problem was the fault of the aggrieved citizen himself. In these ways the Guards usually managed to avoid any interaction with the public or provide them with any service.

To justify his position, Staple moaned about the complexities of drawing up the weekly rostra of officers' shifts, which only death or conflagration could make him change once it was pinned it up. He hid his lack of management skills by retreating behind piles of paperwork which he generated himself. Paperwork did not answer back. He was quick to inform Captain Fletcher about late reports, untidy uniforms, or any other minor lapse, so the pair were able to convince themselves they were doing a good job.

And now they had to convince others, because the Chief Inspector had announced he was shortly to pay a visit. The Inspector was usually miles away in Midgarden. But he'd received reports criticising the way his guards in Diamare were carrying out their duties. There were accusations of bribery. Fletcher suspected it was that martinet in Dom Rei, Captain Bell, who'd tipped off the Inspector.

Fletcher was under pressure, and he was going to save his own skin. That meant doing something about discipline and claims about backhanders. Or getting rid of officers who didn't toe the line.

When Vallora, Dogpole, and Mopper returned to the Guardhouse, Staple was waiting, his prominent nose flushed with anticipation. He sniffed smugly and said Captain Fletcher wanted to see them. They hadn't exchanged a word since leaving their lodgings, and the silence continued as they took the stairs to Fletcher's office.

The Captain was pacing the room. He frowned at them before sitting ponderously behind his desk.

'I have not called you here to answer complaints about your unauthorised changing of duty shifts, or your continual grumbles about designated patrol partners, or, indeed, your gambling,' he said, listing them anyway.

'No, sir?' said Vallora politely.

She was always punctilious. In fact, she was so painstakingly correct when she spoke to him, it sounded like mockery. The young officer at her side stifled a snort and then quickly assumed a wooden expression. Fletcher resolved to stamp his authority on the interview.

'You were seen near Cooper Street. In cahoots with a suspicious...'

'In a what, sir?'

'Hobnobbing,' Captain Fletcher said irritably. 'With a ruffian from that nest of thieves in The Stews. I've reason to believe he was involved in the robbery at Honest John's Discount Bling. The witness says you were engaged in conversation with him, and that afterwards you took him to your own lodgings, he believes to conclude some sort of deal. This looks bad, very bad indeed. He believes money exchanged hands.'

Vallora stood frozen at the charge of bribery, and clenched her jaw so hard the scar on her cheek stood out white against her olive skin.

Mopper stepped in front of her to the desk. 'This witness was Staple?' She thought she'd seen him standing outside their lodgings. Now she was sure.

'*Officer* Staple brought this to my attention, as a matter of fact,' Fletcher said, rattled that his deputy had been observed.

Mopper nodded. 'He was outside on Peat Street all the time we were questioning the suspect.'

'He's a snout,' said Dogpole.

'Staple is a...? Is this a dig at the Deputy's unfortunate…?

'The suspect is a snout. A snoop. A snitch—'

'Get on with it! What about the break-in?'

'We was tryin' to persuade the little runt…the suspect…to give us the name of the brains behind the theft. He was nervous about bein' seen talkin' to us. So we took him off the street. In pursuit of our enquiries.'

'You don't think Deputy Staple would've stood by doing nothing, if he'd thought officers were accepting bribes?' said Mopper.

Fletcher knew that was exactly what his deputy had done. Staple thought he'd found a way of getting rid of the three of them. Instead, he'd been rumbled. Fletcher stared at them in frustration. He'd have to accept their glib explanation for the moment. But he was going to have strong words with his Deputy.

***

They'd been running away. The reevers had swung bolases round their heads and thrown them, and the corded weights had entangled their legs. They'd been brought down like animals. Crossbow bolts protruded from their backs. After they'd fallen, they'd been beaten and kicked. Someone had hacked off the hair of one of them as a trophy.

The Aelythir stood in silence. Alfyndur knelt to close the staring eyes and bowed his head, but no sign of grief or rage marred the chilly contours of his ageless face.

The Aelythir carried their fallen comrades to their deep caverns. Alfyndur laid his hands on the earth and spoke words of protection. Briars pushed through the soil and covered the bodies in an impenetrable shield.

When Alfyndur rose, his face was implacable.

\*\*\*

The guards were in The Carter's Arms, tucking into a supper of leek and potato pie swimming in gravy as thick as porridge. Grilled turnips had been used as a substitute for meat. The tavern won no plaudits for the quality of its dishes, but was popular on three counts: the food was cheap, it was filling, and there was plenty of it.

Mopper had done a double shift, and her knee twitched in complaint. Vallora took it for granted she would always have her back, but a word of thanks would have been nice, she thought. Under the table, she surreptitiously stretched her leg. Her companions were unappreciative of her efforts. Vallora had, in her high-handed way, pledged their help to Tripp without feeling the need to consult either of them. Dogpole was a pragmatist. He'd go along with Vallora if it meant escaping the Guardhouse for a few days. Did they ever consider *she* might have an opinion?

Mopper looked up to Vallora. She admired her, and tried to copy her. She knew she still had a lot to learn. But her companions could be patronising because they were so much older, she thought resentfully.

Vallora broke the silence. 'Maybe I shouldn't have made Tripp that promise. It's just that...'

'You're bored,' said Dogpole.

'You can laugh, but it isn't only that. We *don't* forget old friends.'

'Old friends?' said Mopper. 'You haven't spoken

36

more than two words to Blaise!'

Vallora smiled. 'But I have it on excellent authority that he's a good sort. He helped us back at Old Hall. I'm not going to turn my back when he's in trouble. Are you? It's the right thing to do.'

'You don't get prizes for doing the right thing,' muttered Mopper.

Dogpole gave a mocking laugh. 'So young, and so cynical!'

'Don't talk down to me!'

He grinned. 'Well, it'll be difficult to—'

'Don't! Don't say anything clever!'

'All right. I'll leave the clever talk to you.'

She flushed and turned away. Her aching knee was making her crotchety.

Despite her misgivings, she was in Fletcher's office early next morning, along with Vallora and Dogpole. The Captain wasn't pleased to see them, and looked warily at the determined angle of Vallora's chin. But to their astonishment he agreed to their request to pursue enquiries into Blaise's disappearance. Fletcher eyed the letter on his desk from the Chief Inspector announcing his imminent arrival. He was eager for them to set off immediately.

'If you need assistance,' he said, 'apply to the Guards at Touchstone. No point trailing back here.'

They made their way briskly to The Carter's Arms for breakfast.

Vallora said, 'That was unexpected.'

Dogpole shook his head. 'There's summat havey-cavey about it.'

'Fletcher wants to be rid of us,' said Mopper.

'Yes. Let's get going before he changes his mind.'

Mopper was surprised at Vallora's unconcern. 'Shouldn't we find out what he's up to first?'

Vallora paused at the tavern doors. 'It won't be anything good. I can't bring myself to waste time thinking about him after his offensive accusations. But Blaise has been missing for days, so I *am* concerned about him. Absolutely.'

She went to the bar to order breakfast and a packed lunch.

Mopper climbed gingerly over a bench to sit at the communal table. She stared down at its familiar dents and stains, and wondered why the prospect of going on a trail again filled her with foreboding. What had happened to her sense of adventure, she thought? Though she railed against the routine of the Guardhouse, was she afraid to leave the safety of its walls?

Vallora had dealt with their objections in her usual positive manner. Mopper tried for a more confident approach herself.

'We should start at Touchstone market. That's where Blaise was going.'

'Come on, Kat! You can do better than that!'

Mopper flushed at Vallora's dismissive tone. She went back over the information Rafi had given them.

***

After breakfast they rode north cross-country to Old Hall. Dogpole relaxed as soon as they left the guardhouse behind. The fresh air brought a sparkle to Vallora's eyes. Mopper couldn't resist a gallop at Crouchstone Downs, but then slowed her lively mare so as not to exhaust her. They alternated trotting with walking their horses, and made good time over the plains, reaching the house at sunset.

The balmy autumn was reluctant to leave Old Hall, and a mellow warmth lingered on its walls. The rambling mansion had been undergoing restoration to its crumbling masonry and leaking roofs. The rooms of the main house smelled of freshly plastered walls. The builders had moved on to repair the fire-damaged tower, and Lady Melissande had turned her attention to the gardens.

The travellers found her outside with her steward, Hobbs, and her uncle, Lord Natchbold. Melissande wanted to pick their brains about how the estate had looked in her parents' time. She had recently employed two assistants for Shaw, the gardener. They were all in the orchard, looking critically at the heavily-burdened fruit trees and overgrown pathways.

Lady Melissande welcomed her visitors warmly. She was reassured to learn they were taking on the search for Blaise themselves.

'Because nothing is more important than family and friends.' Melissande beamed at everyone with such affection that Hobbs had to clear his throat. 'We're all worried about Blaise. Poor Mistress Jessup is distraught.'

Melissande and her uncle had recently returned from the Free Isles. Their visit had been happily prolonged for several months while Hobbs organised the most disruptive of the building work, and they had returned buoyant and refreshed. Lord Natchbold was a little plumper, Melissande marginally thinner. Her curls, which had bleached to a strawberry colour in those sunny islands, were smoothed into thick loops on the nape of her neck. She had adopted the flowing dress of the islanders, which emphasised her generous curves. The critical Priss thought the style 'foreign'. Mistress Jessup informed her sharply that it was 'very becoming'.

Enjoyable as it was to renew old friendships, there was nothing useful to add to the information about Blaise that Rafi had already discovered. So the next morning, Vallora and her friends took the road to Touchstone. A mile beyond the town was a straggling village with houses and shops strung either side of the street. A small brass plate caught a ray of sunshine.

Mopper leaned from the saddle.

'Here! This must be it. Hepworth and Tremble, Lawyers and Agents.'

Mopper's second thoughts about where to begin their search had prompted her to remember the description of the seal on Blaise's letter. The scales indicated a firm of lawyers. Blaise had been on foot. In Touchstone they found out the only lawyers within walking distance were in Outlane. It seemed a reasonable place to start.

Dogpole pulled at the bell rope. A doleful note echoed inside. They waited. Dogpole was about to tug the rope again when there was the sound of footsteps descending from the floor above. The footsteps paused. Dogpole put his ear to the door. He heard wheezing. After a minute the footsteps began again, making slow progress down the hall. On the other side of the door, bolts were drawn back, and there was the chink of chains as a padlock was unlocked. The door creaked open a crack. They adjusted their eye-level. A small man with a starched collar and wispy white hair stuck his nose round the door.

'Yes?' he said.

'We've been sent by Captain Fletcher of Diamare Guards,' said Dogpole. 'We're enquirin' about one of your clients.'

The man turned round and started back up the hall to the stairs. Before he'd gone four steps, Dogpole pushed the door wide open and reached out to pull him back. The little man hung limply, swaying on the balls of his feet. Then he felt himself being lifted level with Dogpole's chin.

'Where're you goin'? We been standin' here ten minutes. We ain't standin' here for another ten.'

'Sir! Please let me down!' He was shaking. 'I was going to fetch young Master Hepworth.'

'Let me guess,' said Mopper. 'You're Mr. Tremble.'

'Oh, no, miss. Mr. Tremble is quite an *elderly* gentleman, miss...'

'When you've finished your chat, we have work to do,' called Vallora. She was already climbing the stairs. 'And Dogpole? *We're enquiring about a client?* That'll get short shrift here.'

Young Master Hepworth was seventy years old. He wore spectacles on the end of his nose. To see who had barged into his office, he raised his eyebrows, tilted back his head, and squinted down through the lenses.

There were three City Guards. One was a tall young woman with remarkable silvery-grey eyes. If the lawyer had been of a fanciful nature, he might have described her eyes as the colour of a winter sea. But he was not a fanciful man, and just thought she looked like a cold fish. On her left was a younger girl of average height, with fair curls and an affable expression. To her right stood a rangy, tough-looking officer rolling a toothpick round his mouth. His face was scarred, part of one of his ears was missing, and he needed a shave. He looked like the sort of character against whom clients brought charges of grievous bodily harm.

But the lawyer was used to dealing with Guards

and officers of the Merchant Watch. For years he'd deflected their ponderous questions, run rings round them with legal jargon, or cited 'client privilege' and refused to answer. He gave a tight little smile.

'Good day. How may I assist you?'

'See, you got this wrong,' said Dogpole. 'You got the wrong end of the stick right there, pally. Boot's on the other foot.' He closed the door with a click and leaned against it.

Vallora looked at the lawyer coolly. 'You are the one in need of help, Mr. Hepworth.'

She put her hands on her hips, which drew attention to the handcuffs and truncheon hanging from her belt.

Mopper adopted a curiously clipped manner. 'Captain Fletcher has sent us to bring you in. He believes you are involved in a case of kidnapping.'

Hepworth was so shocked he sat up and pushed his spectacles to the bridge of his nose.

'*Kidnapping*?' he gaped. 'Are you *serious*? This is preposterous! You can't believe...I am a *lawyer*, madam!'

'And I am an *officer*, sir. Not a madam. A madam is something quite different. Absolutely. I advise you to choose your words with more care.'

Mopper planted her hands on her hips and regarded the lawyer's bald patch and frayed cuffs with freezing disdain. Vallora looked startled and Dogpole shot Mopper an apprehensive glance.

Mopper took some papers from her tunic. 'Let's see…Complicit in the disappearance of one, er, Breeze…Braize Pilger?' She peered at the paper. 'Pilgin? No…Pegrim…Blazer Pegrim…'

'For the gods' sakes! Mr. Pilgrim? Of *course* he wasn't kidnapped! It's absurd! You're wasting your time and mine. I should like to know who—'

Mopper interrupted. 'No-one's seen Mr. Pilgrim since he visited you. We suspect kidnapping. Or worse.' She folded her arms, lifted her chin, and fixed him with a haughty stare.

Vallora had been watching this performance with a horrified eye. Dogpole stepped forward.

'Where are you hidin' 'im?' He opened the doors of a wall cupboard.

Vallora moved round the desk, and tried the handle of one of the drawers. It was locked.

'I want all the keys to this building,' she said. 'Is there a cellar? A floor above this?'

Dogpole rifled clumsily through the shelves, and the lawyer got to his feet.

'Please, leave that cupboard alone! There are important papers…This is nonsense! It's obvious I wouldn't hide anybody in there!'

Three pairs of eyes swivelled round to him.

'Where *would* you hide a body?' said Vallora.

'I didn't mean…Mr. Pilgrim left this office perfectly well. He was in good spirits, and—'

'From the beginning, sir.' Mopper stared at the lawyer with such intensity her eyes began to water.

The boy who'd presented himself in response to the letter was a good deal younger than Hepworth had expected, which had increased the lawyer's reservations about having taken on the business in the first place.

'Your grandfather was…enigmatic.'

The boy had looked a question.

'I mean he gave very few details. Other than that you are in danger and must leave at once.'

'Leave Old Hall?'

Hepworth wondered if Outlane was as far as the boy had ever ventured. But he'd been paid to pass on the instructions, so he ploughed on.

'Your grandfather believes it isn't safe for you to return. He wants you to join him immediately.'

He unlocked a drawer in his desk and withdrew a purse.

'For travelling expenses and anything you need on the way. A most generous gentleman, your grandfather, but in a hurry. He believes you are both in danger.'

The boy's grandfather must have sidelined the doorkeeper, because he'd arrived unannounced. Hepworth had not heard his approach. But there he stood in front of his desk, a slight fellow with peculiar eyes. Importantly, carrying a great deal of money.

Hepworth had excused himself so that he could

examine the coins and count them. He'd even bitten some of them, to make sure they were genuine. They were old coins, pure gold. The lawyer's office, hidden away in this village, had the sort of clients who didn't want to attract attention. The man was not his strangest-looking customer. He was by far the wealthiest, and the lawyer had been reluctant to turn him away, however odd his instructions.

Hepworth reached into the drawer and took out a bundle folded in linen. The boy unwrapped it and stood turning a pendant over in his fingers. He looked very vulnerable.

'You're not obliged to do anything, Mr. Pilgrim. I must admit, I have doubts about this whole business, as I indicated in my letter. It is highly irregular.' Hepworth fidgeted under the boy's blue-eyed scrutiny. 'To speak plainly, I think it would be reckless to leave your home without a word to anyone, travel so far, and alone, in these troubled times—'

'Will you tell me how to find him?'

The lawyer regretted his choice of words. He had hit on exactly the sort of phrases which would encourage a young man to set out on some foolhardy adventure. He sighed and shook his head.

'Don't worry, sir,' Blaise had said kindly. 'I'll be all right.' He smiled.

And the lawyer, under the spell of that magical smile, had been willing to believe him.

*** 

Outside the office, Dogpole exploded. 'What in blazes was *that*? "Braize Pilger...Breezer Pegrim?" What if he'd asked to see the papers you was supposed to be readin' from? It was embarrassin'. I didn't know where to put meself!'

'It worked, didn't it? He admitted Blaise had been there. He'd have clammed up if we'd asked him direct.'

'That pantomime was an impression of me?' said Vallora.

Mopper was on the defensive. 'I was playing it by ear. Like you do. Why is it all right when *you* do it, and wrong when I do exactly the same thing?'

'I wouldn't try anything so risky with a lawyer.'

'You looked as if you were off your head!' said Dogpole. 'You only got away with it because Vallora and me distracted 'im!'

He might have been more sparing had he not been in a bad mood, and his mood had nothing to do with Mopper's questionable tactics. Their visit to the lawyer had been successful. They knew where Blaise had headed. But Vallora had announced the direction she thought they should take to catch up with him. Dogpole thought her decision foolhardy. Escaping the Guardhouse on this jaunt had suddenly become a less pleasant prospect.

'It'll take twice as long by road,' Vallora said, in

anwer to his objections. 'Blaise has the march on us. Absolu—' She bit back the word and sent Mopper a frigid look. 'Time is of the essence.'

They reined in at the little stone inn by the mill near the West March. The last time they'd braved Withy Woods, they'd barely penetrated its outskirts. Vallora's route meant they'd have to cross right through it.

Mopper shifted in the saddle. She was afraid that in her wish to prove herself in the lawyer's office, the only thing she'd demonstrated was ill-judged rashness. Her companions were scathing about her lack of experience. And though she always brushed off questions about her knee, it had never fully recovered from the fight at Old Hall, and she was worried it might make her a liability. She eased her leg in the stirrup and looked towards the woods. It was an unusually warm day for late autumn, with clear blue skies, but the forest was sunless and sinister.

'They say no-one walks willingly into the realm of the Fair Folk,' she said.

'Who does?' said Vallora.

'It's a saying. People say it.'

'Not in Mohavia, they don't. In Mohavia they say 'Tell me an old wives' tale and I'll tell you ten that contradict it'.' Vallora dismounted and unstrapped their bedrolls. She hoisted them onto her shoulder and shot Mopper a challenging glance. 'I don't take scary stories on trust. Do you?'

She crossed to the inn, ducking under the arch of its doorway.

'Well *I* don't like the look of it,' said Mopper. 'I like a road. A road and a map.'

Dogpole's roan snickered as if she agreed. He ran his hand soothingly down her neck. 'You know what I think of forests. Suffocating hindrances.'

He lifted a coil of rope from the saddle horn and clipped it to his leather belt, next to the scabbard holding a long-bladed knife. Then he unbuckled the saddlebags.

'It's on foot from here. Horses are no use in that terrain.'

Mopper dismounted reluctantly, and he caught her uneasy look towards the woods.

'Safety in numbers! Nothing ventured, nothing gained! There's some more sayin's for you! Come on Kat, you're a match for anythin' you'll find in the Withies!'

He turned to follow Vallora, but she stopped him with a hand on his arm and looked earnestly into his face. 'Do you think so?'

He looked down at her quizzically. 'You make *me* nervous.'

'Be serious for once!'

He paused before responding lightly, 'Oh, I am. Breeze Pegrim? Braize Pilger? That was a worryin' moment.'

'Thanks. That helps no end.'

The innkeeper looked anxious at their entrance.

But they weren't asking questions about illegal moonshine. They wanted stabling for their horses, and were offering generous payment.

'How long for?' He folded his arms, refusing to touch the bag of coin.

'For as long as it takes,' said Vallora.

She dumped a second bag onto the bar. He loosened the cords and looked inside. His eyes widened.

'Fair enough,' he said. 'For that they can eat at my own table.'

The guards were equipped for a journey. He asked where they were headed, and then made the gods' sign.

'I wouldn't go into the Withies! There's evil men hiding there. And there's pigwidgins and bugaboos, and the Fair Folk, which is the worst of the lot. I can tell you stories would bring you out in a cold sweat. People disappear!'

'So I've heard,' said Dogpole. 'But we've made a few people disappear ourselves.' He grinned and leaned over the bar. 'Take care of our horses, okay? Then you won't have to worry about no-one disappearin'.'

He slapped the innkeeper heavily on the shoulder. The man flinched and swore he would look after their horses as if his life depended on it.

'You said it, pally,' said Dogpole.

They paused to fill their water bottles at the mill leet, before crossing the road into Withy Woods.

***

Sessile followed Fraya to the Thrones' Room. Her stately progress was like the slow shifting of sand, the irresistible movement of roots, or one rock settling on another.

Volte, Bretth and Lorelai were already seated at the table with Oculus, who looked harassed. Umbra was noticeable by her absence.

'You all agreed,' Oculus was saying. 'How about a holiday, I said. Good idea, you said.'

'We may have agreed to a holiday,' said Volte. 'Not to an eternity twiddlin' our thumbs! And whose idea was The Retreat? What sort of a name is that?'

'He's got a point,' said Bretth. 'Sounds as if we've abandoned them.'

'But we *agreed*...'

Volte flared up. 'So you keep sayin'! But *some* of us are pokin' about in places they shouldn't!' He slammed his fist onto the table. Sparks leapt into the air.

'He means Umbra,' said Bretth helpfully. 'She's leaving shreds of night all over the place. It's interfering with the Scrying-Glass.'

'Is she upset?' said Sessile.

Lorelai tossed her head. 'Never mind Umbra, *I'm* upset! She's covering the forests in perpetual night. I can't bring dawn there because she keeps them in darkness. But no-one cares how *I* feel! It's

51

all about Umbra!'

'Withy Woods is under shadow. What are you going to do about it, Oculus?' said Aquaphraya.

'Looking out for Westerburgen, as usual?' said Oculus, trying to shift attention. 'I thought we'd agreed. No favouritism.'

'I've never made a secret of my fondness for the Riverlands. But this is about *you*, Oculus. While you and Umbra have been indulging in your little tiff, you've let things slide.'

Bretth sighed. 'I remember when we used to take an interest in Seywarde.'

'I *liked* it when we got involved,' Volte said belligerently.

'Yes,' said Oculus, 'but by and large, *they* didn't.'

'What are you sayin'? That mortals are better off without us?'

This interesting question was not investigated, because at that moment, Sessile, who absorbed things more slowly than the others, stirred.

'Darkness over my forests?' An indignant flush mounted her noble face.

*In Pairika, the Silverhead mine shuddered.*

'Everyone to the ladders,' the Seamline Foreman said abruptly. His voice had such an odd note that the miners turned, their hammers and chisels suspended. 'Leave the tiffin, Dosenwyse.' He pushed the dawdling dwarf ahead of him.

They clambered to the surface and screwed up their eyes at the daylight. All now heard the creaking which had alerted the foreman. Beneath them, rock walls vibrated, and scaffold props buckled and snapped.

The Earth goddess was slow to anger, but once roused, her anger ran deep.

*** 

The trees grew close together, rusting leafcover shutting off daylight. Roots burst through the soil, and twined with other roots to trip them. There were hollows treacherously filled with water.

Vallora, Mopper and Dogpole pushed through ferns which soaked their boots, and thorns which tore at their britches. After an hour they found a clearing, clumps of nettles and bracken growing through the ashes of an old campfire. It was very still and quiet.

Dogpole felt as if the trees and bushes were watching, seething with anger at their intrusion. He split some fallen timber with a broad-bladed knife like a cleaver. He shaved off curls of wood and when he'd gathered a heap, coaxed them alight with sparks from a chunk of flint. Vallora nipped off the young leaves of some nettles and put them in a pan of water heating on the fire, along with dried beans and pearl barley from their supplies.

Mopper squatted down and gave the pan a stir. Dogpole leaned over her shoulder.

'Take over if you want. I don't know anything about cooking,' she said.

'No, you're OK.'

'Why are you hovering, then?'

'It could do with some onions.'

'We don't have onions and you're still hovering.'

'We passed wild garlic on that bank.' A recollection from her farmwork jogged Vallora's memory. 'You could use that instead.'

'Garlic?' said Dogpole.

'Mm. Those plants with ragged white flowers. The leaves have gone yellow but…'

'Sounds appetisin'.'

'Make do, then! We can get a meal in Fallowdale.'

Dogpole glared at the enclosing trees. 'That's dandy! Only there ain't no signposts, an' I swear them bushes keep movin'.'

'We don't need signposts. I can smell out water. Once we find the Blackwater, we'll cross into Fallowdale.'

'Well, if you follow the river you can't go far wrong,' said Dogpole.

He turned his head. He took two strides towards a thicket and pulled out a figure who'd been crouching there. It was a grubby little girl with tangled hair and a mouth stained with berries.

'What're you doin'? You spyin' on us?'

'Put it down for goodness' sakes,' said Vallora. 'It's only a baby.'

'No I en't. I'm nearly five,' said the child.

'Nearly five, eh?' said Mopper. 'Where are your parents, pet?'

The girl eyed her speculatively. Ignoring the others, she walked over and sat close to Mopper.

'I'm hungry,' she said. 'I en't eaten all day.'

'Dear me. You can have some soup, if you let me wipe those berries off your mouth.'

The child allowed Mopper to clean her hands and mouth. Vallora smiled, bemused at the ease with which Mopper struck up conversations.

Dogpole muttered, 'Never mind soup. She wants a good talkin'-to, is what she wants.'

But he went over to the steaming pan. The girl watched his every movement. Dogpole rationed out the broth into tin mugs and cut up a loaf from one of the satchels.

'Where have you come from?' said Mopper when they'd finished eating. 'Are you lost?'

The little girl stuck her fingers in the mug for the last drop of soup, licked it off, and shook her head.

'If you ain't lost, you can be on your way,' said Dogpole. 'And so can we.'

He stamped out the fire. The girl got up and edged closer as he began packing up their bags. He looked down at her.

'You got your soup. Now out with it. Where are your parents?'

'I ain't got no parents. I'm a norfan.' She turned large brown eyes on him.

Dogpole was unmoved. 'So am I.'

She was startled for a moment, and then said suspiciously. 'No you en't. You're too big.'

Before he could be inveigled into an argument, another voice intervened.

'Give it back, our Thelma! You're such a liar!' An older version of the girl emerged crossly from the trees. She came to a halt in front of Dogpole, looked up at him nervously, and pulled her sister away.

'Don't take no notice of her mister, she's tryin' it on. Dad'll give you such a whippin', Thelma. I been lookin' for you for ever.'

'But there was blackberries,' whined the little girl. 'Don't tell on me, Francie!'

'Give what back?' said Vallora, seizing on what she saw as the important point.

Dogpole picked up the girl and swung her upside down so that she dangled by her ankles. A knife and a tin mug clattered to the ground.

Mopper, embarrassed, replaced the blade in her boot and picked up the mug. 'Clever.'

Thelma smiled at her pityingly.

'I hope you're clever enough to find your way home,' said Mopper. She looked up through the trees at the darkening sky. 'And I hope you don't run into any boggots on the way.'

She smiled with satisfaction at Thelma's scared

expression, hitched the satchels over one shoulder and joined Dogpole. 'Coming, Vallora?'

Vallora picked up the bedding. 'Look, we've got to go. Can you find your way back?'

''Course,' said Francie. She looked around and pointed vaguely north.

'You'll be all right, will you?'

''Course,' said Francie again. 'I always look after our kid.' She took hold of her sister's hand.

'Good. That's very good.'

'Come *on*,' called Mopper.

'Right,' said Vallora.

'What's the hold up back there?' Dogpole's voice drifted from the trees. 'You said we'd be in Fallowdale by suppertime. Get a move on!'

Shadows were already swallowing Mopper and Dogpole. Vallora thought it couldn't be later than three o'clock in the afternoon, but here darkness had already fallen. A yellow mist began to curl up from the ground. It wrapped round the trees and gave the impression they were moving. Vallora shivered. It was an unfriendly place. Perhaps she should have listened to her friends' reservations about taking this route. She looked down at the small faces turned up to hers.

There was a crackling of leaves and pine needles and the sound of heavy footfalls. The girls turned to the noise and clung to one other. Dogpole barged into the clearing, followed by Mopper.

'What's goin' on?' he said. 'Why are you still here?'

'We can't leave them,' said Vallora.

'What d'you mean? Sure we can. They'll be fine.' He looked across at the little girls. 'You'll be fine, right?'

'Yes, mister,' Francie said quickly.

'There you are, then,' said Dogpole.

'We can't leave them here,' said Vallora. 'They won't find their way back on their own.'

'And we will? They know their way round here better'n us.'

He looked at Francie's quivering chin and Vallora's folded arms, and got a sinking feeling. The prospect of comfortable lodgings in Fallowdale was rapidly fading.

'Damn it, Vallora! We agree a plan—well, *you* agree a plan and we go along with it. We work out all the details, and then you get side-tracked and the whole thing goes arse over elbow! An' that's the truth of it, ain't it, Kat?'

'Yes, but don't swear,' said Mopper.

*'What?'*

'Don't swear in front of the little ones. Take these saddlebags, will you?'

'Why the...?'

'Take the bags! Vallora, give him the bedrolls. We'll carry the children. Francie, tell us the way.'

***

They were being followed. Their trackers circled silently, so that their stealthy movement might have been trees, disturbed by a gentle ripple of wind.

But Dogpole was aware of the figures appearing momentarily, on the edge of sight. He used evasive tactics, plunging deeper into the forest, veering off at an angle between a stand of alders, doubling back to clamber over boulders, ploughing straight across shallow streams and up slippery banks.

Vallora and Mopper followed, their movement hampered by the little girls clinging to their backs. They pushed through waist-high bracken to a patch of turf encircled by gloomy cedars. Their branches were woven together overhead like an upturned basket.

Dogpole dropped the bags and moved away to scan the darkness beyond the cedars. Mopper took the girls to sit against a tree. She took off her coat and draped it round them.

'Stay quiet,' she whispered. 'Not a word, mind.'

A crossbow bolt thwacked into the turf near her feet. A shadow emerged, carrying an axe. On the opposite side of the clearing, light glinted off a blade as a man stepped from the trees. Too late, Dogpole realised they'd been herded to this spot. With a roar, he ran at the knifeman, grabbed his arm and spun him round. Rather than have his shoulder dislocated, the man had to follow his arm round. Dogpole felled him. He turned to see Vallora crouched, her blade held out at arm's length,

Mopper at her back. They shifted round, as more men and women arrived until they were surrounded. The threatening figures made no move to attack. They simply stood under the encircling trees, watching.

Vallora wondered what they were waiting for, when she found herself pinioned. A net, thrown by men hidden in branches above, had descended on her. Immediately, the people in the circle rushed forward and secured it to the ground. Vallora and Mopper scrabbled underneath, trying to use their knives to cut through the ropes, but the net was too constricting and they got in each other's way. Before they could make any headway, cloths soaked in some foul-smelling oil were shoved over their noses and into their mouths.

Vallora coughed and spluttered. 'Run, Dogpole! You heard, godsdammit! Get out while you can!'

Dogpole ran. The last thing he saw was Thelma and Francie, carried by two of the ruffians, being taken away at speed through the trees.

***

A horned moon rode the mist and looked down on the Aelythir gathered to raise their hands in nightly greeting. Four men skulked in thickets, watching. One of them sniggered. Another spat and sneered, 'Dokkalfar! They stink of the Netherworld!'

60

Two fitted bolts to their crossbows. The others tightened their grip on clubs. As they moved forward, a creature sprang from the ground behind them with such speed it was difficult to register more than a whirl of limbs. It appeared to hover in the air, while the movements of the men below seemed unnaturally slow and sluggish. The figure gave a savage cry of rage and stabbed down again and again. When he stood, his eyes were blazing and his mouth bloody. He stalked past the Aelythir and disappeared into the brooding dark.

***

Dame Chance had a selective memory, for which she was thankful. Being forgetful was a benefit in her line of work. She tried to remain indifferent, whatever accidents befell mortals when she turned the cards or cast the dice. But she couldn't help noticing that when she rolled for Blaise, the die turned up six. Every time. Which was perplexing.

She wondered if she'd inadvertently accepted an invitation to be a godmother at his naming-day. Had she hung over his cradle, and bestowed on him the gift of good luck?

***

Blaise's background was vague. His mother had brought him to Touchstone when he was a baby, from where, no-one seemed to know. Those who remembered her described her as stand-offish. That she 'kept herself to herself' might have been none of her choosing. The townsfolk looked down their noses at anyone who hadn't been born there, and could prove that generations of their family had been born there as well. Mother and son were left very much to themselves.

And then, a few years after she'd arrived, she presented herself one wintry night at Old Hall with her child. She had to leave urgently for a time, she told the steward. She knew no-one in Touchstone to whom she could entrust her son while she was away. Lord Natchbold was a benevolent man, she said, known to have taken in children needing refuge. If she could only speak to him, she was sure he would not turn away her boy. She looked anxiously at Hobbs.

'Lord Natchbold isn't here,' he said.

Just as well, he thought. He could imagine his lordship's apoplectic face if requested to house another waif and stray. He was already guardian to his niece and his ward, and disliked the position so much he rarely visited.

Despite this, Lord Natchbold had the reputation of being a philanthropist. Countryfolk who lived nearby believed his crabbiness was the result of an unhappy love affair. He had never married, and this, together with his wealth, was enough to persuade them that he spent his money on charitable causes. When he was overheard being brusque with a neighbour, they would nudge each other and say, 'Ah, but *underneath*, you know, he has a heart of gold,' and look fondly after his retreating figure. Lord Natchbold's retreating figure was large and uncompromising. Nevertheless, they would often add, 'Underneath that fierce exterior, he's as gentle as a lamb.' And they would exchange knowing nods.

The country folk had strange notions. They were notoriously perverse. For instance, they believed in the existence of vampires and the Fair Folk, although none, to their knowledge, had ever met one.

Hobbs regarded the young woman doubtfully. She seemed dismayed to hear of Lord Natchbold's absence. She had a delicate, bird-like frame, and skin of a warm, coppery colour. Her hazel eyes, as they rested on him, were flecked with golden lights. Hobbs looked down at the bewildered boy clutching her skirts, and hesitated. If Lord Natchbold had the reputation of being a kindly man, it was not his place to undermine it. It was a cold night to turn anyone away.

He consulted the housekeeper. Margery Jessup was resolutely unmarried but had a soft spot for children. She was generally described as 'a fine figure of a woman'. It is the description you apply to a handsome but formidable female of whom you are a little nervous. Her appraising eyes took in the mother and child. The young woman was neatly dressed. The little boy shone with good health. He looked up at her with a trusting expression, and gave a smile which pierced her heart. To her surprise, she found herself sweeping him into her arms, and planting a kiss on his plump cheek.

'He will be safe with me. I give you my word.'

Hobbs was startled by this unexpected response, but rallied with admirable composure.

'Madam, if Mistress Jessup gives you her word, it is as good as set in stone. Mistress Jessup's word is the law here.'

'Thank you!' said the woman. 'I won't forget your kindness! Be a good boy, Blaise.' She whispered a few words in his ear, kissed him, and hurried away into the night.

Next morning, Hobbs and Mistress Jessup held a further conversation. In the cold light of day, they wondered how they'd been charmed by a woman and child they knew nothing about. They decided it was best not to bother Lord Natchbold with the details. In fact, they didn't have any details, so they didn't correct those who assumed the child was being minded by the housekeeper for some relative.

But as days went by, and then weeks, Hobbs and Margery Jessup reluctantly concluded that the boy's mother wasn't coming back. They'd had no word from her. Perhaps she had never intended to reclaim him, and their instincts had been wrong. Perhaps some accident had prevented her from returning. But as the months passed, what was certain was that Blaise flourished under Margery's care, and was the apple of her eye. They were inseparable.

One frosty dawn when she went out to break the ice on the pump, there was a dish of strawberries on the kitchen doorstep. Hobbs found her with Blaise on her lap, sharing the fruit. Hobbs had come to show her a bottle left at the front door.

They presumed the gifts had been left by Lord Natchbold. They'd grown used to his eccentricities. He didn't like Old Hall, but would arrive without warning, and expect that his apartment was prepared and a fire lit by the time he'd drunk his first glass of brandy. It was an imposition on the overstretched staff but it appeared that, despite his gruff manner, he appreciated them.

'Strawberries in winter, Margery?' Hobbs said.

The fruit was fat and juicy, and smelled of warm summer fields. He opened the bottle and poured them glasses of amber wine.

Margery sipped appreciatively. 'Very pleasant. A bit like elderflower.'

They toasted Blaise. Coincidentally, the gifts had been left a year to the day the little boy had been brought to the Hall. They chose to celebrate it as his birthday. It was as good a day as any.

It appeared that Lord Natchbold had forgiven their subterfuge, and had accepted Blaise as part of the household. So Blaise grew up in the kitchen, smiling his irresistible smile, beaming trustfully at Mistress Jessup whether she scolded or indulged him, which she did in equal measure.

No-one knew how old Hobbs was. He'd been the Hall's steward when Melissande's parents were alive. Lord Natchbold, nominally the head of the household until his niece was of age, kept him on. Hobbs looked much the same as he'd always done, middle-aged and quietly efficient.

Margery Jessup, too, changed little over the years. Her energy did not diminish, nor did the sharpness of her tongue. Her chestnut hair, combed into a severe bun, was thick and lustrous. The years passed, but the colour did not fade.

***

Hepworth had given Blaise directions to a post house on the West March Road. Unaccountably touched by his interview — possibly he liked being addressed as 'sir' — the lawyer had taken time to scribble down a list of items the boy might need on his journey.

Travelling by coach was time-consuming, but the alternative was crossing Withy Woods on foot, and the forest was inhabited not only by murderous bandits but the perilous Shydd. The lawyer was a countryman. He believed the woods were the realm of the Fair Folk.

The West March was an old military road which ran from the south to Burlap, where it split west to Riversholm, east to Kenfig, and became the Great North Way as it advanced through Nordstrum. Hepworth told Blaise he should take a stagecoach to Burlap and then a local carriage west. He didn't know exactly where Blaise's grandfather's cottage was, except that it was somewhere in Greenwood Forest near Bowsprit, so it would be Shanks's pony from there. The lawyer thought the journey would take two days, or two and a half, depending how soon Blaise could find a stagecoach going north.

After he left the lawyer's office, Blaise returned to the market. He was familiar with the local stallholders who brought produce to sell in Touchstone. There he invested some of his new-found wealth in a change of clothes and some other necessities, and a backpack to carry them in. A hopeful tradesman, seeing that he had money to spend, tried to tempt him with a cherry-coloured velvet jacket with brass buttons. Blaise consulted the lawyer's list, and opted instead for a long green coat of thick worsted cloth. The high collar helped disguise the bulge of the purse hanging round his neck. He slipped the coat on over his shirt and jerkin.

He was fortunate enough to get a lift to the West March in Bosky Brownleaf's cart. The farmer was returning to his smallholding a couple of miles from the road, but Blaise was such a sympathetic listener that Bosky offered to take him all the way. As they drove along the winding country lanes, Brownleaf grumbled about the difficulties facing farmers: sheep with foot-rot, cabbage white-fly, lazy hired hands, the weather, and the stinging rates levied by Touchstone council on stallholders.

By the time they parted company, the farmer had unburdened himself, so was in good humour, and Blaise was at a small inn next to a watermill, from which he could see the road north. Across it was the forbidding darkness of Withy Woods.

Blaise stepped onto the West March with some trepidation. A twenty minute walk brought him to a post house, The Travellers Joy.

 The yard was crowded and noisy. There were ostlers leading away horses, and travellers pushing into the post house to find food and drink before fresh horses were brought.

Swirling dust and the sound of horns heralded the arrival of coaches, and slamming doors and warning cries their departure. New travellers were issuing instructions to coachmen, who strapped their luggage onto the roofs, while passengers inside were leaning from the windows calling for refreshments. Several times Blaise was shouted at, because wherever he stood he was in the way of someone bustling about on urgent business.

He crossed the yard to the hostelry, a two storey

whitewashed building with chimneys. There was a public eating area, and private parlours with fires for wealthier travellers. It had a large staff, for it provided stables and grooms for horses, as well as bedrooms for two-legged guests.

Blaise wondered how he would find a coach to Burlap, and who, amongst the men in green aprons and women in white aprons he should approach. He was knocked into and tutted at by people who had a job to do and a pressing timetable to keep. Blaise, dithering by the door, nervously fingering the heavy purse under his coat, was an annoying obstacle in a fraught day.

It was a confusing place for a boy used to the sedate life at Old Hall, where he was surrounded by familiar faces, and one day was much like another. And it might have gone very badly for him, for in crowded places with bona fide travellers there are also bona fide card-sharps, conmen, pickpockets, and similar fleecers of gullible people with money in their pockets.

A middle-aged man got up from a nearby table, where for the past two hours he'd been nursing a half-pint glass and scanning the room. He wore a jacket thin for the time of year, short at the wrists and shiny at the elbows.

'Good afternoon, *monsieur*,' he said, addressing Blaise with a plummy accent and an oily smile. 'Forgive my intrusion, but may I offer you somewhere to sit out of this crowd?'

He took Blaise's arm and steered him to a table.

'You are not a regular traveller, sir? I myself do a great deal of travelling in my capacity as, er, *Bureau* to the Duke of Burgunda. But, *pardonnez-moi*! I digress! I am currently *en vacances*, and am at your disposal.'

Blaise understood enough of this to know that this kindly person was offering to explain the workings of the post house and would be able to show him how to get a ticket for the stagecoach. He was obviously well-connected, well-educated, and an experienced traveller, although Blaise wasn't sure what a *bureau* was. Probably a steward, like dear old Hobbs.

The man introduced himself as Ricardo Chisel. He said it was fortunate that Blaise had found him, because coachmen took advantage of solitary passengers, and post houses were notorious for overcharging their customers. Blaise would be advised to leave the organising of his journey to someone *au fait*, like himself. Blaise was grateful, and told him that he was going to visit his grandfather, who lived near Bowsprit. He handed over a substantial amount of money to secure a chamber for the night and a seat on the next day's coach to Burlap.

Presumably on the way to take care of these arrangements, Mr. Chisel came across some friends hanging about the yard. They were grim-looking men who looked as if they were seldom amused, but he captured their interest by telling them a story about a pigeon who was asking to be plucked. After some conversation, they shook hands and the men rode off.

When he returned, he invited Blaise to join him for supper, which he ordered with such ease that Blaise was impressed. Several hot dishes arrived, together with a jug of ale and two bottles of wine, and the waiter presented the bill. Unfortunately, Mr. Chisel was embarrassed to discover that he had left his purse locked up with his luggage in his bedchamber. But this minor snag was easily overcome, as Blaise assured him that he had plenty of money to pay for the meal, and promptly did so.

They chatted amiably. His new companion insisted that Blaise call him Ricardo, as he already felt they were firm friends. He said he intended to take the young man under his wing. The wine flowed—into his *own* glass, because, he said in a fatherly manner, it was his duty to make sure Blaise was clear-headed for his journey next day.

The evening continued merrily until midnight. Blaise exclaimed that his new friend's anecdotes about his travels were as good as the adventures Mistress Jessup used to read to him, about a young woman who spun stories to delay her execution. Mr. Chisel smiled and spread his hands modestly. Seeing the boy was yawning, he said Blaise ought to settle his stomach with biscuits and milk before turning in for the night. Ricardo promised to keep him company, and make do with the house's pork pie and cheese, washed down with more ale.

Blaise obligingly called a waiter over. At which point, the landlord himself took an interest…

There were branches of the Jessup family all over Seywarde, and all were involved in catering or management, as housekeepers, innkeepers, or Major Domos. Less industrious and successful folk said the whole family was by nature bossy. And if that means they had a flair for organising people, that was true. The sugar of the pill was that they were also attentive to the comfort of the people they so ruthlessly managed. None more so than Jens Jessup, who had run The Traveller's Joy for the past fifteen years, ever since he was a shrewd young man of twenty-five.

He'd been making sure that all the guests, animal and human, were fed and watered and stowed for the night with the minimum of fuss. He was now at leisure to take a hand in attending to the few customers who remained in the public dining hall. Which was when he heard his name, and saw Blaise. And his companion.

It emerged that Mr. Jessup knew Tricky Dicky. The money Chisel had extracted from Blaise had not been used for the coach or a bedchamber. It was in his pocket. He was swiftly ejected, with the minimum of disruption to the other guests.

Jens was one of Margery Jessup's nephews, and she'd always been a kind, doting aunt. The family did not often get together, being too busy to take many holidays, but when they did, Blaise figured largely in her conversation. So when Jens laid eyes on Blaise and heard him mention her name, he put two and two together and knew he must be the 'tow-haired lollop of a lad' his aunt spoke of so affectionately.

Jens was mortified that someone so dear to her had been scammed by a crook under his own roof. He returned the stolen money, and packed Blaise off to bed, promising to set matters to rights before he laid his own head on a pillow.

Next morning a neat young man in a green apron roused Blaise with hot water, soap, and towels and withdrew while he washed. He took Blaise to a private parlour for breakfast, where he waited on him without any apparent haste, although he kept one eye on the clock.

'Mr. Jessup regrets that he is unable to attend you himself this morning, sir. I hope the eggs were to your liking? If you are ready, I will take you to your coach.'

The neat young man accompanied Blaise to the courtyard, which was already a bustle of comings and goings, and led him unerringly towards one of the stagecoaches. He told the coachman that Mr. Jessup would be obliged if Mr. Pilgrim had every comfort on the journey, and was put off the coach at Burlap.

Then he settled Blaise inside with a travel rug and

handed him a packed lunch.

'Mr. Jessup apologises for the inconvenience you suffered last night. Goodbye, sir. Thank you for your custom.'

Later, when Jens found time to speak to him, the young man reassured him that Blaise had been sent on his way with the utmost discretion. Jens looked with approval at his son and hoped he'd done enough to prevent Aunt Margery getting wind of Blaise's visit.

***

He was known as Monsieur de la Roche in Midgarden, Balefire in Southron, Thimblerigger in Westerburgen, and The Pied Man in Nordstrum. In Diamare's underbelly, they called him Jack the Flash. It was here in The Stews—known to its inhabitants as The Paradise—that people went to disappear. And Jack might have disappeared for good when the fireworks in his shop caught alight on Patty-Cake Day and burned the building to the ground.

The narrow lanes of The Stews had heaved with holiday crowds watching the pudding race, when plumcakes heavy as lead were bowled along the streets. Afterwards the guisers had put on the play of Bold Slasher and the Dragon which always went down well, partly because everyone knew the words and you could buy bags of raisins to pelt the Fool, and mostly because the tavern keepers supplied liberal amounts of free ale all day.

At dusk, rowdy singing accompanied a torchlit parade through the streets to the bonfire, and then flaming brands were thrown onto a mountainous pile of wooden pallets and broken bits of furniture, and there was dancing and drinking round the fire.

Things often got out of hand on holidays, what with the torches and drunken fights. People were injured and buildings were damaged, or vanished altogether, leaving streets looking like a set of teeth with a molar missing. Such things were hardly remarked on in The Stews, but Raphael Tripp had been there that night and had watched the Magic Shop burn down with Jack inside it. At least, that's what he *thought* he'd seen.

Rafi had been three or four, peeping at the parade from behind a pair of legs like temple pillars, when everybody was startled by a rumbling sound, followed by a thunderous clap as a burst of fireworks shot into the air.

At first the crowd oohed and aahed, thinking the display from the Magic Shop was part of the celebrations. Spinning wheels burst into dandelion heads before falling to the ground. Fiery red snakes fizzed and leapt, snapping over Rafi's head. There were feathery plumes of witchy green, and a screech of rockets which dissolved in showers of golden sparks. And then, with an explosion of blinding white light, the roof of the building erupted in flames, and a deafening blast shook the street. A cloud of sulphurous smoke descended, smelling of gunpowder. People started shoving and yelling as fire leaped to the neighbouring shops, and Rafi was knocked to the ground. The pair of legs had bent, and he'd been picked up from the cobbles to join the flight from the inferno.

So he was surprised when, visiting Em years later, he saw the owner of the Magic Shop in Touchstone, wearing the same striped hose and patchwork coat, and looking much the same, but smaller. Or perhaps Rafi was just bigger. He was curious, and when Raphael Tripp was curious he asked questions. He was good at ferreting out information.

He was currently ferreting through the clothes of a well-dressed stranger lying unconscious in an alley off Cheese Crust Lane. Rafi cut the straps of the purse from the man's belt, and then rifled the pockets of his coat. He glanced at his companion, a portly fellow lounging against the wall cleaning his nails with a knife. A billyclub hung from his belt.

'You didn't need to hit him so hard, Badger.'

The man shrugged. 'He's a tourist. Fair game. I done him a favour. He'll wake up with a sore head an' he won't wander the Paradise again.'

'No, not without protection,' said Rafi. 'Not in this waistcoat. But I meant he was probably going to fall down anyway.'

He gestured to the flamboyant yellow garment. The man had eaten one of Ye Olde Deli's pasties, and had compounded the error by washing it down with a bottle of Ye Olde Speckled Goat. Evidence of the effect on his stomach was plastered all over his lurid waitcoat.

'You done?' Badger was impatient. 'Toss us the purse.'

'Hang on!' said Rafi.

In his coat pocket, the tourist carried a booklet entitled 'The Sites and Sounds of Olde Diamare.' On the front was a drawing of a charming, picturesque street with higgledy-piggledy houses.

It bore no resemblance whatsoever to The Stews, and, since it was in black and white, had avoided any hint of those colourful aspects for which the area was notorious. The author had taken the idea of artistic licence and galloped off with it.

'Listen to this!' said Rafi. ' "A quaint historic gem. Explore its cobbled lanes and investigate its ancient trades and ec…eccentric characters".'

'He done that, all right. He can tick that one off. Stop foolin' around, Rafi. Hand over the purse.'

But Rafi was looking at a soft blue pouch of fine leather. 'What have we here?' He weighed it in the palm of his hand. 'Pretty, isn't it? And heavy. Feels like…' The contents chinked gently against each other. 'I dunno. Marbles? Little pebbles?'

His companion gave up cleaning his nails, and pushed himself away from the wall, an arrested look in his eyes. He looked again at the tourist's expensive clothing.

Rafi was examining the pouch. 'It's been sewn up. I can't open it. I wonder why he would—'

'Chuck it over!' Badger was suddenly alert. The knife, no longer an instrument for casual manicure, was held threateningly towards Rafi. 'Now! No more messin'.'

Rafi stood up, his eyes wide. 'Hey, come on, Badger, old friend. *I* found it. Fair dos. Share and share alike. We're both—'

'A pint in The Jolly Cleaver don't make you a friend. Throw me the pouch, sewer rat, or I'll give *you* a knock on the head. Wanna try me? Toss it over!'

Rafi took a frightened step back. He threw the pouch and scarpered.

His aim was poor. The bag landed a few yards behind Badger, in the vile-smelling detritus of the alley. Badger swore and scuffled around for it. He wiped the pouch on his tunic. The hard contents ground against each other. He had to squint to see the small stitches securing one end. He tried to prise them open with the tip of his knife, swearing again when the blade slipped and caught his hand. The cut bloomed red and he jerked his hand away. In frustration, he poked at the pouch, trying to slit it open, but the leather was resilient and sprang back. Eventually his efforts ripped open a tear and the contents spilled onto the ground.

He dropped to his knees in the dirt and scrabbled about, glancing up and down the alley, fearful now. There would be other streethawks on the prowl. He picked up some of the gems and rubbed off the muck. A reddish one. A blue lapis lazuli. A cluster of sparkling crystal chips. A stone with yellow and brown bands like a tiger's eye. But wrong. They all felt wrong. He weighed them in his hand and turned them over. Then with a roar he hurled them away. Felt like little pebbles, did they? That's precisely what they were.

Meanwhile, half a mile away in one of the dark ginnels frequented by sewer rats, Rafi strolled along munching a cheese and onion pasty. It wasn't from Ye Olde Deli. Those pies were strictly for tourists, although they had an interesting crunch if you were in the mood for adventure. Rafi knew the only pies worth eating were from Aggie Butter's veggie-stall by the laundry. He'd given up buying anything in The Paradise described as 'meat' since Sleazy Todd had choked to death when someone's ear had found its way into his liver pasty.

The tourist's purse was a satisfying weight in Rafi's coat pocket. He mused on the gullibility of people in general, and of the slow-witted Badger in particular. Because Rafi had visited Honest John's. After hours. The shop was stuffed with bright and breezy trinkets: rings with stones of startling hues, bracelets of shiny yellow metal, and chains with vividly-coloured pendants. Their composition and colours proved them to be cheap imitations aimed at the poor or credulous. After a few days, the stones faded to colourless paste, the rings turned your fingers green, and the chains brought you out in a rash.

Rafi was feeling pleased with himself, but was startled out of his complacency when a man appeared in front of him. He couldn't see where he had come from. There were no shadowy doorways or entrances to narrow alleyways on this stretch. Rafi was too astute to have dropped his guard had that been the case. Nevertheless, a man had materialised from somewhere and now faced him.

There was nothing in the least remarkable about him. His features were instantly forgettable. He had studied the art of being inconspicuous and passed with flying colours — the colours being unrelieved black. Rafi's stomach lurched and the pastry turned to dust in his mouth.

'Good evening, Mr. Jackson.'

'I 'ope you're right, Rafi,' whispered the assassin. 'Optimism should be cherished like a delicate whossname. Flower.' The poetic Mr. Jackson gave Rafi a glimpse of the stiletto under his cloak, and jerked his head for him to follow.

Rafi dragged after him in mounting panic. What offence had he committed that he should attract the attention of an assassin? As they drew nearer Heaven's Gate, which was the entrance to The Paradise, they emerged into a wide street. It was somewhat confusingly called Via Principalis, since it was a cul de sac. At its end, it opened out into a large square, around which were imposing buildings, including guild houses. Temples, some of them brand spanking new in red brick or pristine sandstone, jostled for space. Amongst the oldest buildings, the Temple of the Indistinct Mystics of Umbra wavered into view from time to time, and then disappeared, leaving the hazy afterglow of a silver cupola.

It was an area Rafi avoided, since it was the most wholesome part of The Paradise, with the cleanest beggars, best-dressed thieves and politest assassins.

The guilds had armed doorkeepers to make sure it stayed that way. In contrast to those forbidding entrances, the House of the Vestals had a welcoming red light above its open doors. Under its rosy glow stood a giant of a man with a fluff of hair around his bald head.

'Evenin', Brother Smalls,' said Jackson. 'Evenin', William,' he added to the corner of the building. A boy in various shades of black and acne slid from the shadows, looking sheepish.

The doorkeeper held out a hand resembling an old leather bag. Rafi felt about in his pocket and took out some coins. William sniggered. Brother Smalls shook his head. Rafi reluctantly drew the knife from his belt, and placed it on the man's palm. The doorkeeper continued to hold out his hand. Rafi sighed and rolled up a leg of his britches to remove a second knife strapped to his calf. This was eventually followed by a jemmy from an inside pocket, a skeleton key hanging round his neck, and a razor from the peak of his cap. The doorkeeper frowned.

'I never taught you nothin' about razors, Rafi. You 'ent clever enough not to cut off your own fingers, and a dipper needs 'is fingers.'

William sniggered.

'Get off 'ome, Billy,' whispered Jackson. 'You 'ent old enough to be 'anging round the Vestals.'

William blushed and scampered off.

Rafi followed the assassin through the doors and

gaped at the opulence inside. Lamps cast subdued light on the hall's painted walls. There were plaster statues of satyrs, and nymphs holding armfuls of fruit. On either side of the room were pillars, behind which were upholstered sofas in red velvet. This afforded some privacy to the couples engaged in intimate conversation. Elsewhere were gilt chairs at tables where some of the occupants played cards and dice. The men were fashionably dressed, as were the attentive ladies looking after them, though they seemed to find the room too warm for any but the lightest of garments.

At the end of the hall stood a table filled with bowls of sweetmeats: candied fruit, turkish delight, coconut macaroons, sugared almonds, marchpane, chocolate drops, caramels, violet creams, peppermint ice, and pink marshmallows.

Motherly ladies carried in trays of drinks Rafi had never seen before. The slender stems of the glasses held flutes bubbling with brightly coloured liquids decorated with cherries on sticks and little paper umbrellas.

A young woman approached them, smiling a welcome. Rafi took off his cap.

'Good evening, Mr. Jackson. Supper will be served shortly. May I offer you something to drink?' Her warm glance embraced them both.

To Rafi's disappointment, the assassin shook his head. 'We're 'ere to see Miss Surplice, Peri.'

'Of course. If you would wait a moment?'

She made her way unhurriedly towards stairs leading to some upper chambers. Rafi looked on hungrily as plates piled with savouries were carried to the tables. What a very relaxing and comfortable place this was!

Mr. Jackson, however, looked neither relaxed nor comfortable when Miss Surplice appeared on the stairs. Possibly because she was not alone. She was saying goodbye to a graceful young man with curly hair, who bowed over her hand and left her regretfully, to console himself with sandwiches.

Flimsy Surplice was a dainty vision in celestial blue, which exactly matched her eyes. She glanced at the room below to make sure that all her guests' requirements were being religiously attended to by her sister Vestals. Then she smiled down on her two visitors.

As he followed her up the stairs, Rafi was in the enviable position of being able to admire at close hand her slender waist and swaying hips, brushed by a shining fall of platinum hair. He was being invited to supper by an angel! They sat down and she apologised for keeping them waiting.

'Business, my love,' she murmured to Jackson.

She turned to Rafi with an enchanting smile.

'Mr. Tripp, what a delight! So kind of you to come. *Do* try the pastries. And some fresh salad? It's *so* important to stay healthy, isn't it.'

Rafi had been helping himself from the dishes

brought by one of the kind Sisters, while he took in his surroundings. The salon had a thick carpet his feet sank into, and deep armchairs cosily arranged in front of a fire. Mirrors gleamed in the firelight. The room was fragrant with vases of fresh flowers.

The door to a bedchamber was ajar, and Rafi caught an enticing glimpse of a large bed with silk draperies, and a tumble of garments on a chair, all ribbons, frills and lace. Everything around him was soft, warm, and inviting. Like Miss Surplice herself.

And then his innate shrewdness reasserted itself. '*So* important to stay healthy.' He had not been invited to supper by the delightful Miss Surplice. She had sent an assassin to fetch him.

'May I call you Raphael, my sweet? Now, I hear you have been asking questions about a *very* dear gentleman, who is a *particular* friend of mine. You are *such* an observant boy, my pet! Isn't he, Mr. Jackson? So clever! *So* many questions! But my very dear friend would rather *not* have attention drawn to him and his whereabouts. Do you understand, Raphael? And his friends would think you impolite—and imprudent—to make further enquiries. You would not want to embarrass me, or indeed Mr. Jackson, would you, poppet?'

Rafi, a little pale, assured her that was the last thing he would do.

'It would be,' agreed the assassin.

Rafi collected his belongings, and Miss Surplice

accompanied 'Goodnight' Jackson outside.

'Nightie-night, Flimsy,' he said. His voice held the hint of a question.

She glanced at Rafi thoughtfully.

'Oh, I don't think that will be necessary after all, my love. Raphael Tripp has a highly developed instinct for self-preservation. Our mutual friend has nothing to fear from that quarter.'

There was a barely perceptible movement as something was returned to the folds of Jackson's dark cloak. Flimsy paused on the steps to blow the assassin a kiss. Rafi, oblivious of his escape from a short, painful (although exquisitely executed) death, gazed wistfully after her.

'I suppose Miss Surplice has a lot of very dear friends.'

The assassin confirmed that this was an accurate assumption, although he didn't look particularly happy about it.

'Miss Surplice is very beautiful, isn't she? I think she is quite perfect. And very persuasive. And charming. And so...' Rafi came to a halt, unable to find the words to describe her impact on him.

Mr. Jackson smothered a sigh. 'She's all that.'

***

Dogpole ran, Vallora's steely voice in his ears. They'd been outnumbered. Better if he remained free to effect a rescue when the opportunity came. Vallora could track water. He could track people. He could read prints on the ground, however faint.

So he ran. When he was certain no-one was in pursuit, he slowed down. He lit a cigarette while he figured out what to do next. He'd dropped the bags and bedrolls back in the clearing, and now only two satchels remained, slung crosswise across his body. He had nothing to dig with but his knife and his hands, but he did his best to bury the satchels in brush, close to a twist of the Blackwater where it ran through a hawthorn brake. The spot was marked by a tree with a split trunk. He would recover the bags later.

He glanced up at the stars to keep a grasp on his bearings, but the trees got thicker the further into the woods he went, and obscured the sky. Forests were alien to him. With the onset of night, retracing his steps and picking up the bandits' trail would be difficult. Dogpole knew he would be fighting the suffocating feeling of being enclosed.

He began to imagine that the wood was trying to imprison him. Black birch trees grew so closely together their scaly trunks were thin and twisted. The withered remains of catkins hung from the branches and showered him with rank pollen as he pushed through. Trails of creeper tangled in his hair. He forced his way through thickets of gorse.

The uneven ground was slimy with rotting leaf-mould.

The air was heavy and humid, as if the trees were sucking out all the air. The further he went, the harder it became to breathe. Mud pulled at his boots. He'd stepped into a bog. Puffballs rose from its scummy surface and broke against his clothes, releasing a nauseous gas. There was a chittering sound in his ears. He shook his head to clear it.

Bindweed obscured the ground. He couldn't see where to step. He put his right foot down. There was nothing there. He fell into space and landed heavily, wrenching his ankle, before tumbling down a bank. There was a pool at the bottom of the slope. He slid to a stop, hitting his head on some boulders, and lay half in and half out of the water.

There was a sour smell. Faces swam before his eyes. Children. The pungent smell grew stronger. Children with grubby faces and wild, dishevelled hair. Thelma and Francie? They prodded at him, chattering. His head was thick. He muttered, 'Are you lost?' There was laughter. He drifted into unconsciousness.

***

Everything about the bandits' camp was temporary. It was frequently moved, to outsmart the Marcher Lord's patrols. A few braziers burned and lit makeshift tents strung between the trees.

Some men and women looked up as two prisoners were taken past.

It wasn't usual for prisoners to be brought to their den. Travellers were bludgeoned, stripped, and left where they were found. Perhaps they were there to have information about the patrols beaten out of them.

Mopper had given away her greatcoat. Vallora was without hers, too. Their knives, truncheons and boots had been taken. They'd come to, groggy from the evil-smelling gags. The bandits had hauled them to their feet, blindfolded them, and shoved them forward.

When they reached the camp, the blindfolds were taken off. To one side of a clearing, poles had been driven into the ground to form a rectangle. Three of the sides were draped with strips of cloth and animal hides, and branches had been thrown on top to make a roof. From them dangled long braids of hair, like scalps. Underneath sat four men and a woman.

Vallora and Mopper were forced to their knees. One of their captors spoke to the seated outlaws. He returned to the prisoners and ripped off their gags. He gave Vallora a crack across the jaw. She hadn't made the journey easy for them.

The people seated under the canopy were as dirty and ragged as the others. A bearded man in a fur cape appeared to be their chieftan, judging by the way the others glanced at him to gauge his reaction. There was a bald man wearing a heavy gold chain, and another with a stump where his right hand had been. On the leader's left was a thin man, his head wrapped in filthy bandages, and a fierce-looking old woman.

The bearded man leaned forward. 'What are you doin' here?'

'You tell me,' said Vallora. 'You had us brought here.'

One of the men delivered another blow to her face. 'Watch your tongue! Next time, I'll cut you!'

'What're you after in the Withies?' repeated the man in the fur cape.

Blood ran from Vallora's mouth. She spat onto the ground. 'Nothing.'

Mopper said quickly, 'We were making for Fallowdale.'

'You were goin' the wrong way for Fallowdale.'

'We got lost.'

'What business have city guards got in Fallowdale?' said the bald man.

Vallora brought up her chin. 'We're not saying anything until you tell us where the children are.'

Their captors stared at them.

'Francie and Thelma,' said Vallora. 'What have you done with them?'

The man with the stump looked at their leader and then said, 'They ain't your concern.'

'And our business is none of yours.'

The ruffian who'd hit Vallora swore and took out

a rusty blade.

Mopper intervened. 'Look, whatever quarrel you've got with us, it's nothing to do with the girls. We were on our way to Fallowdale. We came across them. They're not with us. Let them go.'

'Came across 'em, did you?' said the old woman. 'Stole 'em, more like.'

The bandit chief turned on her. 'Shut yer mouth!' He gestured to the men. 'Take 'em to the cage.'

***

Fighting between mortals was one thing. Infighting amongst the gods was another, and far more dangerous. The rumbling mountains in Pairika made the mines unstable. A sandstorm in the desert almost buried a caravan of traders carrying precious spices from the docks at Dom d'Or. Wildfire chased across dry grasslands in Midgarden, encouraged by a rushing wind over the plains.

Oculus looked blearily round the table and rubbed his eyes. He'd succeeded in distracting his fellow divinities, but they were taking out their frustrations on Seywarde. They looked at him with anger and disappointment. Anger just provokes anger. Disappointment prompts you to examine your failings.

But Oculus was a god, and therefore not keen to examine his failings. He'd been reading 'How to be a Compleat Prince', by Don Alejandro el Viajero. Don Alejandro, a prince of Wyvern House, was admired for his elegant dress sense, skill with poisons, and deadly sword. Those who'd had dealings with him (and survived) described him as a complete and utter prince. Their twisted mouths and acid tone suggested they were being sarcastic. Alejandro had written a lot of useful phrases under the chapter headed 'When You are in A Tite Spot'. Oculus, squirming under the accusing eyes of his fellow gods, thought it was worth a shot.

'I see where you're coming from. I take it on board. I'm open to collaboration on possible initiatives.'

The faces at the table looked blank.

'Er, so let's stick it in the toaster and see what pops up.'

A fiery halo began to form around Volte's dark head. Oculus sighed. It was all very well for Don Alejandro, who only dealt with the politics of mortals. Dealing with divinities was a whole other ball game.

'All right. The…misunderstanding with Umbra has caused problems. I know.' He glanced at Volte, whose hair stood on end with static. 'I'll get on to it right away.'

Umbra was sitting at her dressing table. She had pinned up her hair in an odd arrangement of rolls, and was looking disconsolately at her reflection in a mirror. Oculus, who had been preparing a speech as he trundled along to her bedroom, was thrown off course.

'What in the name of...of Us, are you doing?'

'I've been trying to make it curl. But it *won't*.'

She sank her face onto her arms. Her hair uncoiled and slid about her olive shoulders.

'Whatever for?' said Oculus. He lifted a lock of ebony hair and kissed it.

'You *know* why. Lorelai has such wonderful ringlets, and I thought...'

Oculus looked into his wife's tearful eyes. 'To be plain, Star of My Heart, Lorelai has a habit of shaking her head in my face to get attention, which is very grating. I have always admired dark hair. With no kinks in it. As you know very well.'

'Then why have you—'

'I was jealous. I tried to make you jealous.'

'*Jealous*? Of whom?'

Oculus tried not to grind his teeth. 'Of your cosy chats with Alfyndur. You spend so much time with him. With all his tribe, for that matter.'

She took his hand. 'Oculus, there are so few of them. Fewer with every passing year. It makes me sad to see them so reviled and hounded. I try to protect them, that is all. So they are fond of me.'

Oculus was a little mollified. He made the speech he had practised, telling her, as gently as he could, that the obscuring mist she had cast over Seywarde's forests had not gone unnoticed, and had led to anger amongst the gods.

'I know you don't like us favouring some over

others,' said Umbra. 'But they have become outcasts, when they were amongst the first. I don't want to see them lost to Seywarde for ever. But I will think on what you say. In truth, they are not the easiest to love.'

\*\*\*

They were one of the oldest races of Seywarde, feared by some, hunted by others, forgotten by most.

Long ago they made courteous overtures to the incomers, and tentative friendships were formed. But over time, the Elders saw how easily their trust could be abused and their gifts exploited. They searched out havens far from humankind and warned their people that relationships with such a short-lived race brought sorrow to them all.

Under Prince Alfyndur, those warnings became rules. Any interaction with mortals was punished, but to pursue a love-match meant banishment.

Meredydd had forsaken his people for love of Elodie Fairchild. They enjoyed many happy years together, and the sadness they endured at his exile was lightened by the birth of a daughter.

When Elodie died, Meredydd was inconsolable. Driven from their own worlds, they had made their own world together in Treegarth. He couldn't bear to stay there without her. He wandered Seywarde with his daughter.

It was easy to dupe mortals out of money with charms and sleight of hand, but even gullible folk won't put up with being cheated by a strange fellow in outlandish clothes. Not for long. He was in danger of being run out of every town.

He didn't much care what happened to him, but he had a daughter to raise. He must prepare her for a hard world where love was a weakness that could be used against you, and those closest to you proved the most treacherous.

Meantime they had to eat. He made amulets to sell, and carved flutes out of bone and wood. He put on puppet shows where the marionettes seemed to move without strings. People were mystified and frightened, and stayed away. But they crowded round to watch him juggle with coloured balls, and cheered when he made them explode into golden stars. Meredydd thought he'd got a handle on these simple-minded creatures. They were entertained by loud noises and bright lights.

They didn't like Meredydd. He was an alien, and there was an ancient wildness in his eyes. When they looked at him, they focused on a point over his left shoulder. They felt threatened. There was something condescending in his manner, which made them feel like foolish children. But they put that to one side, because he was selling something they wanted. And they wanted blazing rockets, spinners and whizzbangs, firecrackers and spitting fountains, and screaming scarlet serpents.

Soon he was in demand to put on his dazzling pyrotechnic displays all over Seywarde. And this suited him. He would never have a home here without Elodie. But his daughter was growing. She didn't like the constant travelling. She shied away from strangers, who treated her like a pretty toy, to be poked and stared at. She needed to put down roots, somewhere the odd and freakish found refuge. Meredydd opened a Magic Shop in The Stews.

***

Dogpole was lying on the bank, his cheek pressed against cool moss. The pool was surrounded by willow trees, which dipped their slender arms in the water. He heard laughter, and pushed himself up into a crouch, fearing to see those childlike creatures with their curious fingers. Instead, he saw a girl sitting on the boulders splashing her feet in the water and watching with delight as it sprayed into the air. Then she dived into the pool and disappeared.

He stood up and shuffled to the water's edge. The surface was placid. Becoming anxious, he stripped off his greatcoat and stepped in. The girl rose out of the pool, and shook her hair. She was covered in droplets, which nestled in her curls like pearls and clung to her dress.

Dogpole reached out to her. She hesitated, then

put her hand in his, and they waded to the bank. But he felt no weight as he guided her onto the grass and it didn't seem as if she'd needed his help. Instead, it felt as if she'd conferred a favour. She resumed her seat on the boulder and wriggled her toes in the pool. He couldn't make out her features for the light in his eyes. He was conscious of his torn clothes and the dirt on his face.

'Are you lost?'

He was not sure if she had spoken aloud or if the words formed in his head.

'Yes.' His voice sounded harsh in his ears. 'My Lady,' he added. He thought she smiled.

'Do not be concerned for your friends,' she said. 'Follow the river, and fear not.'

She drew up water in her cupped hands. He watched it run through her fingers, as if it was loath to leave her. Time stopped to look. Some drops fell on him but he couldn't move. When she stood, she blocked out the sky. She leaned down to place the tip of her little finger in the hollow of his top lip.

'Sleep now,' she said.

He slept where he sat, by Fraya's pool.

***

Olwyn missed her mother, and her father had withdrawn into grief and become distant. She felt very alone. She didn't belong in any of the places they visited, and was conscious that she was different to the people they met. Their eyes slid past her, as if they didn't really see her. When their travels took them to Bowsprit, she escaped into the Greenwood, seeking out Treegarth.

Their cottage was dark and uncared-for, weeds growing against the door. She pressed her palms against the familiar barks of the oaks, but they offered no comfort.

She wandered sadly to the bench by the brook, and was startled to see someone already sitting there. A man was staring dully at the water. He was very tall, heavily built, bearded, with thick eyebrows. As if echoing her own misery, he gave a sigh, and ran his hands through his thatch of red hair.

He raised his head and looked straight at her. She stood poised for flight. He held himself still, as if he feared the slightest movement would make her disappear. They remained that way a moment. Then her eyes softened and she gave a tremulous smile. He smiled back at their mutual discomfiture.

She walked towards him. 'I'm sorry I disturbed you. I used to come here myself to be alone, and to think. I am Olwyn.'

He got up, towering above her. 'Orson.'

She gasped and then clapped her hands over her

mouth. 'Oh, I'm so sorry. I didn't mean…it's…'

'I know. It means "bear". I'm told it suits me.'

Her eyes twinkled up at him, hazel flecked with amber light. 'It is a very handsome name,' she said gravely. Her lips twitched with amusement.

He gave a roar of laughter.

***

They lay where they had been thrown, inside a structure of stakes open to the night sky.

Vallora whispered. 'Don't worry. Dogpole will come.'

'Yes,' said Mopper. But she thought, he'd have found us by now. He must have been caught.

The hours crawled by. It began to rain, a thin rain which soaked through her shirt. Her face was pressed into the earth. She was sprawled on her stomach, her hands still tied behind her back. Her wrists felt warm and sticky. They must be bleeding, she thought in a detached way. Her knee spasmed. She was too bruised to move. She sank into an uneasy dream. Dogpole and Vallora lay trapped under giant trees. They called out to her for help but she was mired in mud and couldn't move. A branch fell against her legs...

'Wake up!'

Vallora pushed her foot against Mopper's inert body, and Mopper opened her eyes with a start. There was a shadowy figure at the door of the cage fumbling with the lock. Dogpole! Her heart leapt.

A man came into the cage and looked down at them. It was the grey-haired outlaw with the stump, and he was carrying a knife. Their captors must have decided there was no reason to keep them alive. He stooped over Vallora. Mopper gave a cry and thrashed about helplessly. He turned.

'Quiet!' he whispered. He crouched down. 'If they hear, I'll have to kill you!' He cut the ropes from her wrists and lifted the prisoners to their feet.

'Don't speak!' he said, his face close to theirs. 'You found my girls, thank the gods. They told me you was kind to 'em. Get away from here, fast. They'll kill you come morning. Your clothes are over there.'

He pushed them out of the cage and vanished into the night without looking back. As quickly as their cramped limbs would allow, Vallora and Mopper made for a pile of clothes dumped at the edge of the camp.

'We've got to find the Blackwater. That's what Dogpole will do,' whispered Vallora.

Mopper gritted her teeth and followed. Vallora would sniff out the river. She could count on that.

\*\*\*

In the gloom they made out a bend in the river. On the further bank was a hawthorn tree, the trunk split in two. The water swirled around some white, flat stones which made a crossing point. Vallora waited as Mopper slowly made her way across, and held out her hand to help her up the bank. But Mopper had stopped.

'What is it?' said Vallora.

'I don't know. Look, here. And over here.'

Vallora examined the river bank. Around the deep scores her boots had left in the mud, there were other footprints. They followed them to a straggling thicket. The ground was churned up and covered in the same prints.

'Francie and Thelma?' Mopper was rooting around near the bushes.

Vallora shook her head. 'Not unless they took off their shoes. These prints were made with bare feet.'

Mopper dragged out two empty satchels.

'Well, we know Dogpole was here. What's that noise?'

There was a chittering sound like cicadas or crickets. Then it abruptly stopped, and a brown face peered at them from the hawthorn brake. The face was joined by another, then another. They had dark, tangled hair and feral eyes.

The creatures chattered away in liquid voices. It looked as if they were arguing. Then the bravest of them stepped forward, put a hand to his breast, and bowed to Vallora. He turned to Mopper and smiled. Instinctively, she smiled back. He gestured to her hair, tilting his head to one side enquiringly, and tentatively held up a hand.

She was startled, but saw only naïve curiosity in his expression. He reached out to touch her hair and crooned some words. He seemed fascinated by her pale curls.

The other two, emboldened, drew nearer. One of them pointed towards the satchels and patted its stomach, talking rapidly.

Vallora took a step back. 'Fray's fingers!' she whispered. 'What's that smell? Have you seen their teeth? They're like razors! What in the gods' names *are* they?'

'Whatever they are, now's not the time to ask for our supplies back. Looks like they've eaten them, in any case.'

The creatures chittered together, then the third approached. He raised his palm over his head and made grunting sounds and said, 'Harra loth?'

When there was no response, the one who'd first approached Mopper pushed the others away impatiently. He said carefully, 'Haar thee losth?' Then he put two fingers to his mouth and pursed his lips. He made puffing sounds and grinned at Mopper, and the other two laughed.

'I think they've seen Dogpole,' said Mopper.

She pointed to the satchels, and raised her hand over her head to indicate someone of gigantic size. The creatures nodded and giggled. Apparently they'd found Dogpole entertaining.

'Yes.' She smiled. 'Funny man. Where is he?'

The brave one took her hand and indicated that he wanted her to go with him.

'I'm not sure about this,' said Vallora, as the others approached her and pointed to the trees.

'They seem friendly,' said Mopper. 'I think they know where Dogpole is.'

She stumbled on the uneven ground, wincing at the pain in her knee. Her guide, sure-footed on his bare feet, looked at her in consternation. The other two burst into laughter at her clumsiness.

'They're friendly at the moment because they think we're funny,' said Vallora. 'But gods, they stink like foxes!'

Vallora and Mopper were hustled along on paths they could not see, while their guides kept up a constant twittering. They were slightly-built, barely Mopper's height. Their daring in revealing themselves, and their attempt to communicate, suggested, if anything, the inquisitiveness of youth. Their movements were quick, and their eyes flickered from left to right. Sometimes they halted at some sound Vallora and Mopper couldn't hear, and the one guiding Mopper put his finger to his lips in warning.

They kept close to the trees but the Blackwater was never far away. Leaves had fallen and the ground underneath was slippery. They had been speeding along for some minutes when the creatures made one of their sudden stops. Ahead, what had looked like a patch of shadow, swirled about and lifted to reveal a solitary figure.

He held himself as if he was used to command. There was nothing childlike about him. His eyes were penetrating and proud. There were painted symbols on his face and bare skin. His hair fell to his waist in elaborate knots and braids, held by a copper circlet. Curved knives were in his belt. He wore a necklace made of twisted willow stems woven with leaves and feathers, and a moonstone hung on his breast.

Their guides had fallen to their knees. Mopper knelt too, and pulled Vallora down with her.

The prince stared at them with hostile eyes. He spoke angrily to the kneeling figures, and the bold one answered in his quick, lilting language. They were subjected to another searching look. Mopper lowered her eyes, as their guides had done.

The man in the mist appeared to be communing with himself, or perhaps listening to some voice only he could hear. Finally, he gave a curt order.

When they raised their heads, their guides stood at the prince's side. The mist rose to embrace them. The one who'd befriended Mopper lifted a hand in farewell, and then they were lost to sight.

'Are there kelpies in the woods, after all?' said Mopper.

Vallora squared her shoulders. 'The Blackwater is this way. Come on.'

***

They met secretly in a grove sacred to Oculus, on the outskirts of Touchstone. Its circle of trees reminded them of their first encounter in Treegarth. The shrine was little used and secluded. It had fallen into disrepair when indoor temples became more common. There were weathered steps and a statue of the god, covered in weeds. The stone was chipped and discoloured, moss grew between the god's toes, but flecks of gilding remained on his features and hair. The sun shone on the statue of Oculus and bathed the couple sitting at its feet.

Their growing friendship eased Olwyn's sense of isolation, and whatever sadness Orson had in his own life lifted in her company. After some months, Olwyn decided it was time to tell her father about the bear-like man and their meetings. She ran home, for once careless of the dirt and smells of the dingy streets, and the blank stares of its indifferent inhabitants.

When she reached the shop, she saw her father was engaged in conversation with two men. It was late for customers. The strangers turned at her entrance, and looked at her intently. They made a curiously formal bow of greeting, placing a hand on their breasts, but before they could speak to her, Meredydd said sharply, 'You're late. Go to bed.'

Olwyn flushed at the reprimand and his abrupt dismissal but the visitors fascinated her. They looked so much like her father. She stood at her bedroom door, straining to hear their conversation.

She heard Meredydd say, 'Why now, after all this time?'

The reply was difficult to catch, but she heard 'loss' and 'home'.

Her father said, in that same cold voice, 'If that is true, why did he not come to me himself?'

There was another low response and then her father angrily cut off the voice.

'I have no reason to trust him! Tell my…tell your lord to send no more. You will not find me here again.'

Afterwards, Meredydd was more aloof than ever, and Olwyn wondered how she'd thought she could confide in him. When she asked him about the strangers, he said they were Aelythir from the far havens from which he was exiled. He spoke harshly of their lord, whose heart was set against him. Olwyn wanted to hear more about her kinfolk, but it pained Meredydd to talk about them. She dreaded seeing the lines of grief deepen in his face and shutters descend on his eyes.

When she next made her way to Oculus' temple, Orson was already waiting. He lumbered up from the steps and took her hands.

'Until we met I thought the Fair Folk were a tale for children. And when I'm not with you, I think I must have dreamt you!'

He saw she looked troubled. 'Don't pull away! I'm always afraid I'll say something to offend you, and you'll vanish!'

She shook her head and told him about the Aelythir who had braved the streets of Diamare to seek out her father.

'They wouldn't venture so far on a whim!' she said. 'My father said their lord was set against him, but it seemed to me it was my father's heart that was hard.'

Her words must have chimed with experience of his own, because he rubbed at his beard and said, 'When you exchange harsh words, it's difficult to take them back, and difficult to forgive. And it gets harder with every year.'

'But you should try, shouldn't you?'

He laughed at her vehemence. 'If anyone could bring about a reconciliation it would be you, Olwyn!'

\*\*\*

Dogpole opened his eyes. Willows whispered to each other. While he'd slept, water-crowfoot had sprung up over the pool. Tiny, delicate flowers trembled as the branches stirred the surface. He stretched in the watery sunlight, enjoying the warmth on his body. He felt refreshed, his head clear, his ankle no longer aching.

Then he sat bolt upright. Kat and Vallora. He had only a confused recollection of the previous night. He'd got lost, hunger and fatigue had overcome him, and in the darkness, he'd fallen and hit his head. Nevertheless, he had a strange feeling of exhilaration. He knelt by the pool to dash some water in his face, and looked around.

The pool was fed by a stream, which he guessed was an offshoot of the Blackwater. When in doubt, find the river and get your bearings. He set off, feeling invigorated. Somehow he would find his friends…

…Oculus was playing chess. Sort of. He was out of practise, and the board on the Scrying-Glass was giving him eyestrain. But if he moved *that* piece a smidgen to the right…He stretched his hand to the screen…

*A man found the Blackwater River by falling into it.*

\*\*\*

The coachman woke Blaise at Burlap, and pointed out the inn where he would find a carriage to take him on to Bowsprit. The last stretch of Blaise's journey had been through the night. The coachman warned him local transport was a hit-and-miss affair which offered few comforts.

When the carriage arrived and he climbed aboard, Blaise found the seats were just wooden benches, without enough room between them to stretch his legs. The carriage didn't have any suspension. He took his place between a farmhand who smelled of pigsties and an old man smelling of mothballs. Blaise's knees touched those of a countrywoman sitting opposite, which made him blush.

The carriage started off, rocking over the stony road. In the chilly dawn he was thankful for the travel rug. It had got colder the further north he'd travelled. The purse hanging round his neck bumped on his chest, and he drew the blanket round his shoulders self-consciously.

On his right the ground rose gently to the Barrel Tops. The moorland was scrubby, with patches of white limestone where the soil had eroded. A scattering of sheep chewed on thin grass and thorny shrubs. Some of the flat-topped hills had copses of wind-bent ash and hazel.

The ground fell away on the left to the sheltered valley of Fallowdale. There were barns alongside the road. Beyond, bounded by fences and hedges, fields of green and yellow crops were being cut and gathered into carts. Nestled amongst the fields were farmhouses and outbuildings, with wheel tracks winding to the road.

Blaise was grateful that the package he'd been given contained sandwiches, biscuits, an apple and a small water bottle, though by this time they were warm from having been stuffed in his coat pocket.

The carriage made slow progress, as there were so many stops to pick up and drop off locals at farms or little inns along the way. After a couple of hours, Blaise was weary of the jolting. The carriage jerked to a sudden stop which threw him against the shoulder of a brawny farm labourer. He tucked his legs under the bench in readiness for yet another passenger to board, and wondered how much longer the cramped journey would take.

A guttural voice demanded, 'Stand and deliver!'

Outside was a gang on horseback. They wore battered hats, and scarves covered their mouths and noses. The man in front fired a warning shot. A second waved his pistol at the carriage window.

The passengers climbed out one by one, and stood on the road, shivering in a raw wind. There were five travellers along with Blaise: a student down from university, a mother and daughter—a pretty girl in a straw bonnet with ribbons—and two labourers returning from a week's thatching.

The girl in the bonnet whimpered and clutched her mother's arm when she saw the driver lying on the ground, his face covered in blood…

…Dame Chance sat looking at a boardgame with Grimalkin on her lap. She shook the dice and placed a counter on the head of a snake. A meteor shower rattled along the roof of the Tower of Mystery, and Grimalkin howled despondently. Cassie gave him a comforting scratch behind his ears, but he leapt off her lap and scuttled under the kitchen dresser.

Cassie watched the board. The counter rose as if moved by an invisible hand. It flipped onto its rim and rolled away from the snake's head, coming to rest on a ladder. She frowned, drew a crystal ball towards her, and peered into it…

…The wind sent dirt and grit swirling up from the road, and for a moment the horsemen were obscured. The passengers rubbed their eyes. When the dust settled, the driver sat up, groaning, and applied a handkerchief to his nosebleed.

'Stand and deliver!' The voice sounded lighter and less assured.

One of the labourers ran his eyes over the group of riders, and relaxed slightly. They were younger than he'd at first thought. He calculated he could have all four off their horses in thirty seconds flat.

'Or what?' he said.

'Um, your money or your life?' The rider seemed distracted by the girl in the bonnet.

'Seems a straightforward enough choice. Do we vote on it, or what?' He winked at Blaise.

Blaise didn't see anything funny about being threatened by masked men with guns. His hand crept to the purse, but the labourer frowned and gave a negative shake of his head.

One of the figures spurred closer.

'It's a hold-up,' he explained cheerfully. 'We want your money and stuff. Or, you know, else.'

'Will eggs do?' said the woman.

'We'd prefer cash, if it's all the same to you.'

'I've got two dozen eggs. And a bit of cheese.'

Another voice from the group piped up. 'What sort of cheese?'

'Shut up, Eugene!' said the first masked man. He was growing frustrated. 'Someone better start giving us money, or...well, someone might get hurt!'

To his dismay, the girl in the bonnet gave a sob, and dissolved into tears.

'How dare you frighten her like that!' cried her mother, transformed into a pugnacious figure. 'You should be ashamed of yourself! There, there, he didn't mean it, precious.'

The leader gaped. He was starting to lose confidence in the enterprise. He turned to the rest of the group for support, but his second-in-command shook his head.

'Shouldn't make a girl cry, Tris.'

The second labourer had been lounging against

the carriage with his hands in his pockets, scrutinising the riders imperturbably. They had grey coats with capes, and cravats at their necks. Under their tricorns they wore black masquearade masks. One rider, perched uncomfortably on a skittish horse, had difficulty reaching the stirrups. Another wore make-up, and had applied a thick white line along each cheekbone.

'What's the fancy dress for?' said the labourer. 'Are you mummers?'

The student cowering behind him exclaimed with relief, 'Oh, I know what this is! It's Rag Week! It's a stunt! They're collecting for charity.'

'We're not mummers and it's not a stunt!' said the leader, stung. 'We're highwaymen!'

'*Dandy* highwaymen,' corrected the one wearing make-up.

'Shut up, Eugene!'

The fourth member of the group, who'd been struggling to control his mount, spoke for the first time. 'Dudes! Bogies at six o'clock!'

Thundering towards them was a mounted patrol from Medenhall, the garrison in Fallowdale. They surrounded the would-be knights of the road.

'Drop 'em!'

The weapons clattered to the ground. A soldier dismounted and poked them with the toe of his boot.

'Two potato-guns, one cap gun, and a water pistol, sarge.'

The sergeant's eyebrows rose. He looked sternly at the riders, whose faces had turned as white as the lace at their throats.

'What the hell are you? Mummers? The four horsemen of the bloody awful haircuts?'

'Highwaymen,' croaked the leader.

'*Are* you. Well, sonny, the man in charge of highways round here is the Marcher Lord. You can explain it to him. He won't be happy you've wasted our time. Take the masks off. They ain't helpin'.'

He turned to the patrol, who stared dead ahead with hardly a flicker. 'You two, help the driver up. And then escort him and his passengers to their destinations.' He gave a casual salute. 'Safe journey, ma'am, miss, gentlemen.'

The four unmasked highwaymen had their hands tied, and soldiers took the reins of their horses. The sergeant rode forward to lead the patrol back to Medenhall. He glanced at the prisoners as he passed.

'Tristram? Back from boardin' school already? School terms get shorter and shorter, don't they? Your parents must be thrilled to 'ave you back so soon. Ah, Eugene. Those leather trousers are eye-catchin'. Recruitin' another boyband? I'm not sure about the lipstick. What do you think, Gilbride?'

Corporal Gilbride shuddered. 'Candy pink?' he said faintly. 'With that complexion? Good gods!'...

...'Something's messing with the dimensions.'

Dame Chance left the crystal ball, crossed to a window and leaned out. A trail of stars had left their orbits and were spinning in a circle like a roulette wheel.

'The stars are dancing *In and out the dusty bluebells*. Is Oculus losing his grip, Grimalkin?'

The lizard raised unblinking eyes. He had no opinion about the Optimus Maximus, but he didn't like draughts. He looked meaningfully at the open window. Cassie hummed thoughtfully.

\*\*\*

The river dipped and wound through the wood, and they trailed along, red-eyed from lack of sleep, until they were hailed by a welcome, very human voice.

'Kat! Vallora!' They were enfolded in a crushing embrace.

'Thank the gods!' said Dogpole. 'Ain't you a sight for sore eyes!' He grinned at their grimy faces.

'Thank the gods indeed,' Vallora said. 'You can put me down now, Dogpole.'

He did so, but held on to Mopper and swung her round before setting her down and looking into her face.

'Are you all right?' he said.

'Of course.' She pushed him away. 'Ugh, you're soaking wet! Have you swum down the river?'

'Pretty much.'

They started to retrace their steps, interrupting each other with questions, one minute exclaiming, another silent and thoughtful. Up to this point, they'd had an easy-going attitude to the Pantheon. In other words, they hadn't given it much thought. Fair's fair, one might say. The gods had adopted a similarly detached approach to the human race. But the friends had had experiences they couldn't dismiss as simply the effects of fatigue and anxiety. And they were grateful that they'd found one another so fortuitously. Perhaps, at this moment, they were even prepared to acknowledge the gods' existence...

... *'I'll take that.'* Oculus, watching them in the Scrying-Glass, smiled smugly at their reunion.

And then he saw armed men from the robber camp creeping towards the group. Now, Oculus liked the idea of non-interference, free will, and all that. In theory. He thought it was a good thing, something he ought to encourage. But now he wasn't sure how far he went along with it. Not very far at all, it turned out. The bandits were on the point of bursting through the trees and the friends would be hacked to pieces.

Oculus glanced round furtively. Then he flicked the bandits off the board.

\*\*\*

They were alive. Dogpole glanced at Mopper, who still looked tense. They were bruised, dirty, wet through, but alive. And that was the best that could be said, he thought.

Their supplies were gone. All the things they'd carefully packed as necessities for the journey, gone. He felt about in his pockets and his fingers closed on a solitary coin and a piece of flint. They wouldn't get far on that. They had no weapons, apart from his knife, which hung on his right hip. It was a machete, a cross between a weapon and a tool. The blade was 20" long, broad and flat, wider at the tip. Plates of wood were riveted round the tang to make a grip, but there was no hand guard. The wood was worn and an old repair of twine was bound round a split in the grip. The canvas scabbard hadn't protected the knife from his immersion in Freya's pool. He tried to dry off the blade on his trousers. His greatcoat hung in sodden folds over one shoulder. They were still in Withy Woods. So were the brigands. His initial euphoria faded as they tramped alongside the Blackwater, looking out for a track through the trees into Fallowdale. It began to drizzle, a chill, wintry rain which penetrated the treecover and then their clothes.

The grass on the river bank skidded under their feet. Vallora and Dogpole turned at a cry from Mopper. They hadn't realised she'd fallen behind. She was on the ground, her hands gripping clumps of grass in an effort to stop sliding further down the bank. Dogpole ran back and grasped her wrists to raise her, but she gave a sharp cry and pulled away. She crouched, her arms protectively around her knees, shivering.

Dogpole cursed. He lifted her into his arms.

'It's my fault,' said Vallora. 'I should have realised.'

Mopper's left leg had been put under strain carrying Thelma. She was cut and bruised from falling when the outlaws had forced them to run over uneven ground. Her knee was shooting agonising flames of pain and she couldn't think clearly. She didn't protest when Dogpole lifted her, but hung limply, teeth clenched.

'It isn't sensible to go on,' said Vallora. 'We need to get out of this rain.'

'And find summat to eat.' Dogpole's stomach was rumbling. 'We've had nothin' since that miserable soup you cooked up.'

Mopper tried to smile. Everything ached, even her hair. She was content to be carried, and didn't care where they went, so long as she didn't have to put her feet on the ground.

An hour later, Vallora called a halt and wiped a sleeve across her wet face. 'We haven't found a stick of shelter and I don't know where we are. We shouldn't have left the river. We're drifting further and further into the forest.'

Dogpole looked at a clump of alders growing by

some boulders. Fungus grew on their spotty barks and their black twigs oozed sticky sap.

'You can't tell me *that's* normal!' he said. 'Damn and blast this place!'

'Sh! Don't swear in front of the little one.'

He grinned in spite of himself, and looked down at Mopper. Her head rested just below his right shoulder. 'She's asleep. The sooner we...Where are you off to?'

Vallora had glanced towards the alders, and then her eyes had fixed on the boulders. They were tumbled at the base of a rock smothered in ivy. She squeezed past the boulders and lifted the trailing strands.

'I thought so. It's dry under here. Sheltered by this overhang. What do you think?'

'Anythin' to get out of this rain.'

'Look, it goes further back. I think it's a cave.'

Vallora stooped and moved forward cautiously. Dogpole followed, and when he reached the cave mouth, he set Mopper down on the sandy floor. She murmured in her sleep, but didn't wake. He eased his shoulders and looked around. There was a stack of wood to one side. They weren't the first to seek shelter there.

Vallora's voice echoed back from the tunnel.

'It's getting dark back here. Smells...musty, sharp. I think animals have been in here. It starts to narrow, but I can't see—'

'Vallora!'

She came back at a run. 'What is it?'

Dogpole pointed. There was a shelf at the cave entrance, either a natural formation in the rock or deliberately cut. On it were some shiny, yellowish objects. Vallora stepped closer to examine them. It was a row of skulls.

***

Meredydd wouldn't stay in Diamare after the Aelythir's visit. He stage managed, with help from Miss Surplice and other friends in The Stews, the spectacular disappearance Rafi had witnessed. Under cover of darkness, he and Olwyn moved to a cottage in Touchstone.

The change seemed to make her out of sorts. She lost her appetite and felt too unwell to go out. But she was pleased with the cottage after their dark lodgings. It was light and airy, and when she felt better she threw herself into furnishing their new home. It was a task new to her, and she enjoyed it. 'Nest-building', she thought to herself, and hugged her secret close.

And then, on a day when leaf buds fattened on the boughs and Olwyn felt the first stirrings of the child in her belly, she hastened to the meeting-place. The Three-Eyed god smiled his golden smile, but Orson was not there—not that day, nor the next. She feared her absence had made him think she had forgotten him.

Meredydd did not lose his temper or berate her for her naivety in trusting a man about whom she knew so little. Olwyn thought if he'd been angry it would have shown he cared for her. Perhaps she was too like him, too little like her mother. His eyes only softened when her son was born with the same pale skin and fair hair as Elodie.

Meredydd loved his grandson from the moment he saw him. He spent hours playing with the little boy. He would make stars appear out of the air, and Blaise would kick his dimpled knees, crowing with excitement. Meredydd played funny little jigs on a wooden pipe and Blaise would clap his hands and laugh. Sometimes Meredydd carried him into the garden, solemnly telling him the names of plants and trees, while Blaise burbled and burped, and tugged at the pendant round his grandfather's neck, and stuck sticky fingers in his hair.

And when Blaise was miserable, hot and red-cheeked from teething, Meredydd would lift him from Olwyn's weary arms and take him into the cool night air. He would recite the names of the stars, and sing to the moon, and the little boy would fall asleep at last, soothed by the gentle lullaby.

It didn't last. Meredydd was restless, suspicious of strangers asking questions, and couldn't settle. He began travelling again, selling amulets and potions, putting on firework displays in Southron and Westerburgen. His absences grew longer, and when he briefly returned, it was only to redouble his warnings against the Aelythir. They hadn't given up looking for him, he said. They would try to take Olwyn away, too, and her son. He was convinced his being with them endangered them both.

In the meantime, Blaise was growing into a solid little toddler. One night, when Meredydd was expected back from a prolonged visit to Midgarden, Blaise waited up for him, refusing to go to bed. He stood at the window with Olwyn, looking out at the night sky and a flurry of falling snow. When he saw the figure of Meredydd approaching the gate, he ducked under his mother's arm. Before she could stop him, he had opened the door and pattered out on bare feet. Meredydd laughed, but the air was knocked out of him when Blaise hurled himself into his arms.

In the small hours, as Blaise slept against his chest, Meredydd stroked the little boy's curls. Olwyn knew he was remembering her mother. He told her he had to prepare for a long trip. The mayor of a town in Nordstrum had promised him a thousand guilders to rid them of a plague of rats. He would be away for months.

'Come with me!' he said impulsively.

But his wandering existence had never appealed to Olwyn, and it was no life for a child. And she had another reason for staying. She had begun to piece together details about the man who, apart from her father, was the only person she had trusted. Would he welcome her and her son?

When they said goodbye, Meredydd held her for a long moment. It was such a rare show of affection that tears sprang to her eyes. He pulled away but she clung to him, wondering if he didn't intend to return. His steps were quick and light when he left. He carried only his walking staff and a green canvas back-pack. The wind tugged at the skirts of his patchwork coat and sent a mournful note through the pipe in his belt. He pulled the brim of his hat lower. At the end of the road, he turned and bowed, as the two Aelythir had done, and then he was gone.

She stayed for a moment, holding the hand of her little son. What must it be like for Meredydd, banished from his people and his home? He had been happy with her mother, but for him their time together had been fleeting. Olwyn made a decision she'd thought about for a long time.

***

Vallora and Dogpole stared at the skulls. The skulls stared impassively back at them from empty eye sockets.

'We must have stumbled on one of the robbers' hideouts,' said Vallora. 'I don't think they stay in one place for long.'

'Not a comfortin' thought. Nor is the message:

Keep Out,' said Dogpole.

The cave mouth was filling up with darkness and they could hear steady rain outside.

'I doubt if they'll move in this, not with children. It's hard enough going in daylight,' said Vallora.

Dogpole shuddered. 'Too right.'

'We'll stay,' said Vallora, deciding to take his shudder as assent. 'I don't want to disturb Kat, and I'm dog-tired myself. Let's get a fire going.'

She was already grubbing about under the wood pile collecting wisps of dry grass, leaves and bark shavings. She moulded them into a rough nest shape. Dogpole scraped flakes from his flint into it, and struck the flint with his knife until some sparks ignited and took hold. They added slivers of wood, careful not to smother the flames, and after a while they were able to use twigs, until finally they could put on thin branches from the stack. Before too long there was a cheerful fire going at the cave mouth.

As night drew on and there was no sign of the bandits, Dogpole's doubts about staying receded. They dried their clothes, and Vallora began twisting twigs into an improvised torch, intending to explore the rest of the cave. But she couldn't stop yawning.

When Dogpole came back from collecting wood, he found her lying on the sand under her coat, snoring. He picked up his own greatcoat, now dry and warm, and shook off the sand. He took it over to Mopper and draped it over her. He sat for a while by the fire, smoking, watching the night roll in, and drops of rain sizzle as they hit the flames.

***

Mopper pushed herself up, leaning heavily on one arm. A grey dawn was trying to steal into the cave. She stretched, and was brought up sharp by the ache in her knee. She remembered she'd had to be carried there, and her heart shrank. She'd been right to have doubts about this venture. She was holding her friends back.

Dogpole sat by the dwindling fire. She watched him for a moment, somehow comforted by his stolid shape and capable hands. He was chopping whip-like suckers from a branch of wood. Then she recognised his handiwork and recoiled.

'No! I won't use it! I'm not using a stick again!'

He turned round, startled. 'I thought for now you could...'

'Don't! I couldn't bear it!' Mopper felt tears of self-pity well in her eyes, and blinked them back angrily. She saw she'd been covered by his coat and threw it off.

Dogpole's lips tightened. 'You know what, Kat? You're plain stubborn. You always want to manage on your own. You push people away.'

'I *can* manage on my own! I'm used to managing on my own when...when you go off on one of your walkabouts. Do you think we can't manage without

125

you? I *can*...we can.'

'I know,' he muttered. He scowled at the branch and then threw it onto the fire. 'I know it makes no blasted odds whether I'm here or not.'

She hunched away. 'I hate it when you swear.'

There was a crunch of footfalls. Vallora came from the passage carrying a sputtering torch, and a bundle of firewood. She looked at them, but made no comment on their miserable expressions.

'There's a crate of last autumn's apples. A bit shrivelled, but I couldn't find anything else. I don't think the torch will last to search further.'

Dogpole got up without a word and bent to enter the passage. Vallora heaped wood onto the fire.

'We should make a start soon, Kat. I'll have a look at your leg to see if—'

'Leave me alone. I'm fine. Just give me your hand. I've got to go outside.'

Mopper's palm was hot and clammy. Vallora watched her limp out of the cave.

When Dogpole returned with the crate, she said, 'We ought to go. It's too much of a risk to stay any longer. I wish we could, for Kat's sake. I don't know how she'll manage.' She picked up an apple and stared at it, frowning. 'Her knee isn't any better, but she won't let me help. Does she seem feverish to you?'

'Don't ask me. She don't confide in me.'

'She doesn't confide in me either, but I thought you might have—'

'How will she *manage*? She'll manage herself to a standstill before she'll ask for help!'

'Yes. We'll have to make sure—'

'Especially from me.' He bit savagely into an apple.

'Right. Well, I'm glad the night's rest has put you both in such good humour. I don't think either of you has let me finish one sentence.'

'What?' said Dogpole. His eyes were on the entrance as Mopper hobbled in.

'Nothing.' Vallora shoved some apples into her pockets and stood up. 'Let's make a move, shall we?'

A cold voice said, 'Let's not. I'd prefer you to stay exactly where you are.'

A man's figure blocked the entrance. He held a bow strung with an arrow aimed at Vallora's head.

***

Countryfolk who lived near Withy Woods called them the Fair Folk, and left out bowls of cream at night to coax them into granting favours.

Apparently this worked. Flogg, the shoemaker from Oketon, said the grateful Shydd had come to his workshop after dark, and with their nimble fingers had stitched wonderful leather shoes in a rainbow of colours. As everyone wanted a pair of magical shoes, he was soon rich. Those who couldn't afford them whispered that it was a con; everyone knew Flogg was a tyrant who made his apprentices work through the night. But this may have been sour grapes.

And Ralph, the dunny-cleaner from Windy Bit, said a Shydd had taught his daughter how to spin straw into gold. Which sounds like a good deal for a bowl of cream. He said Lily's gift had so piqued the local baron's interest that he'd married her.

His neighbours were sceptical. They said Ralph, who'd always been a bit strange—and no wonder, considering what he inhaled—had become totally unhinged trying to find the reason for his stunning good fortune. But Lily was a flaxen-haired beauty with a kind heart, and the baron was a cheerful lad with an unpretentious nature, so it was perfectly understandable, and had nothing whatever to do with the Shydd or gold. In any case, they'd never seen Lily near a spinning wheel; she wouldn't know one end from the other. And they all knew she got hayfever when straw was cut at harvest.

All the same, you whispered these doubts behind closed doors, because unlucky things *did* happen if you forgot the cream. Like Dennis breaking his arm doing a wheelie on his dad's cart, and Grannie Crumble's cow getting sick. And things disappeared. Like keys, socks, spectacles, and biscuits. And everyone knew the Shydd were to blame.

Sometimes even *people* disappeared. Harry had disappeared. A Shydd had found him wandering the woods, almost mad with the poison coursing through his veins. The Shydd had sunk his needle-sharp teeth into Harry's wound and sucked out the deadly venom.

***

The stranger's fingers didn't shift on the bow-string but his eyes swept over them and round the cave.

'I'm not used to guests.' He glanced at the skulls. 'Live ones, at any rate. I might get excited and let this loose, so keep very still. I see you've helped yourselves to supplies. I had no idea I was so hospitable.'

Vallora stared into the shadowed face under the hood. She licked her dry lips.

'*Harry?*'

The archer started. A puff of wind lifted a strand of Vallora's hair. She jerked round as the arrow clattered against the cave wall. Then the archer was upon her, one hand at her throat, the other with a knife against her cheek. His eyes bored into hers. 'Who are you?'

A hefty arm wrapped itself around his neck and forced his head back. Dogpole clamped his left hand on the archer's wrist. After a struggle, the blade dropped to the sand. With an almighty effort, Dogpole heaved the man off his feet and fell with him onto the ground, pushing his face into the sand with a heavy slab of a hand.

Vallora picked up the knife, knelt down to slit the right sleeve of the archer's padded tunic, and pulled up the shirt underneath. She sat back on her heels. Scar-tissue ran down the man's forearm.

\*\*\*

He remembered driving his sword through the heart of a murderer. He would never forget that. He remembered nothing about Vallora and her friends' arrival on the scene, nor their attempt to burn out the venom from his enemy's blade. They had been only partially successful. Poison had already leached into his system. He was afraid he would never be completely rid of it.

Some nights he woke in a sweat, shaking, his shirt soaked, a blanket twisted around him, as if he'd been running or fighting in his sleep. And he *did* remember running. Running through the Withies, while disembodied voices called to him and laughed, leading him to stumble into deeper, darker parts of the forest. He thought he must have been trying to seek the safety of his cave, but he didn't get there. Not then.

'I did the best I could.' The girl was looking sadly at his disfigured arm. There were puncture marks near the scar. He rolled down his sleeve and looked into her troubled face, and then at her two companions. It worried him that he couldn't remember them. But he had left so much behind.

130

'You helped save my life, I think. I've given you poor thanks for that.'

When they'd seen his puckered skin, so like the burn marks Vallora carried on her own arm, they knew for certain the archer was Harry. But the man in front of them was thinner and hollow-cheeked. Dogpole thought he wouldn't have overcome the old Harry so easily. Mopper had been nervous of him at Old Hall, and thought he looked even less approachable.

He'd disappeared two years earlier, and Captain Bell, a bloodhound when it came to tracking down felons, had finally concluded that he must have died of his wound. They hadn't known Harry well, but had grieved the loss of a courageous, albeit driven, man, and assumed their efforts had been in vain.

Vallora, like her friends, was reticent about herself, and recognised that there was a great deal he was not telling them. But when he said, 'Harry is dead. They call me Longshanks here', she shivered. Could he really wipe away his past so easily? Could she?

He showed them where they could wash off the grime of the last few days. He took them to a storeroom for duck eggs, salted ham, peppery watercress and cheese. He didn't show them all the cave's secrets. Secrets had kept him alive. Dogpole suspected he had a stash of weapons somewhere.

They told Harry about their visit to Old Hall, but

when they mentioned Melissande he turned away and, feeling uncomfortable, they'd fallen silent.

Later they had bread and jam, and blackcurrant tea. They told him about their search for Blaise. The name didn't mean anything to him, but his eyes glinted at Vallora's description of the bandits' den. She got the impression the thugs avoided Longshanks and his Bone Cave. He said the Marcher Lord had too few men to rid the woods of outlaws. Vallora thought Harry had been rooting them out himself.

They'd been taken off course by the bandits, and their search for shelter had led them further astray. Harry said they were at the edge of Withy Woods, where it petered out at the coast. They would need to go inland to find the Greenwood. Vallora looked round for her greatcoat. Then she saw Mopper was asleep, and that outside it was already dusk.

*\*\*\**

Some time during the night Mopper opened her eyes. She shifted about, mumbling, trying to find a comfortable position, and plucked the blanket away. She was hot and in pain. The man squatting at the cave entrance turned at the sound of her voice. So did his companion. The wolf padded over to Mopper, sniffed, and whined.

Harry rose and went over to look down at her restless form. She stared up with dilated eyes that didn't see him. Underneath the torn trousers, her left knee was red and puffy. Her ankle and foot were swollen. He was surprised she'd been able to walk on it. The wolf nudged at him. He followed her out of the cave and into the wood.

***

The Lord of the Aelythir bent his eyes on the woman in front of him. 'You've been gone all day, Olwyn. You look weary. Where have you been?'

The basket she carried was empty.

'Walking. I've been cooped up so long. I wanted to find flowers to cheer my room, but the Queen's Lace have turned brown, and I couldn't find wintersweet.'

'Cooped up? You are not in prison. You came here freely, did you not?'

'Yes.'

'I have tried to provide for your comfort. What is it you lack?'

'Nothing.'

'You liked the strawberries? I can bring you more, whatever you desire. Is there something you miss? Or someone?'

She avoided his gaze.

'Is there anyone, Olwyn?'

She averted her face.

'It worries me that you go out alone.' He looked again at the empty basket. 'You should not wander from my protection. We are besieged by enemies. Your father would not forgive me if I was careless of your safety.' The bland mask slipped, and he said harshly, 'Your father does not forgive.'

They climbed up the valley side.

'You have had no further thoughts about where his travels may have taken him? No? I will walk back with you.'

He took her arm and they passed under an arch of hawthorn. On an impulse, he stopped and knelt, stretching his hands over the grass. Under his fingers, thin stalks began to push through the soil. The stalks grew leaves and fattened into green buds. When they opened, petals of pure white shone in the dusk. They hung their shy heads like bells.

The prince touched the snowdrops tenderly and smiled up at her. 'A gift.'

She was caught between tears and laughter. He seemed suddenly very young, free of care, delighting in the flowers.

'Thank you, uncle.'

And then, as suddenly, the moment of intimacy was gone. A shadow passed over his face. The shutters had descended and he had withdrawn, as her father did. She thought she'd caught a glimpse of what Meredydd had been, what both brothers had been, before pride and guilt had eaten at their hearts.

'You are a precious gift to the Aelythir, Olwyn.

You must not leave me, as your father did.'

She had come seeking reconciliation. Despite his words, she was a prisoner.

*** 

A creature crouched over the girl's body. It raised its head. Yellow eyes glittered. It spat. And then it was lifted up by its hair and hurled away, and in the same rush of movement, Harry found himself pinned against the cave wall.

Dogpole, his face contorted, said thickly, 'I am goin' to kill you for real, dead man!'

'What's happened?' Vallora stood in the passage, frozen in the act of plaiting her hair, blinking in the pale morning light.

'Devilry! Why did we trust him?' rasped Dogpole. 'What *is* he now?' His hands closed tighter on Harry's throat. 'What have you done to her, you and that vermin?'

Harry's hands flailed at Dogpole's arms, trying to speak.

Vallora ran to Mopper's bed. 'She's sleeping.' She put her hand on Mopper's forehead and looked up. 'She doesn't feel so hot.'

A pad of spagnum moss had been tied round Mopper's knee. Vallora took it off. Underneath, the leg was less swollen and wasn't so fiery red.

Dogpole released Harry, who fell against the wall, gasping for air. When he made as if to join them,

Dogpole put a hand against his chest.

'That's far enough, pally.'

There was a faint chirruping sound. A strange being sat up. It held its head, rocking and crooning to itself. It sneezed and spat into the sand. Then its eyes fastened on Dogpole and it let out a stream of words in a language he didn't understand, but whose meaning was clear.

Dogpole pointed. 'That! That stinkin' little rat! It was crawlin' over her! The gods know what it's done to her!'

'*Look* at her, you fool!' Harry stooped to soothe the angry creature.

'What in the gods' names is it?' said Dogpole. 'It's ugly as hell!'

The creature screwed up its face. 'And thee stho beau-thi-ful.'

'Kat and I saw forest folk like that when we were looking for  you.' Vallora stared at the small figure. 'I think he's one of those who spoke to us.'

Harry said, 'They avoid human contact. You can see why. But I found him close by, and he was willing to help your friend…help Kat.' He still had to fumble for their names. He had little human contact himself. 'I think he was looking for her. He must find her sympathetic.'

\*\*\*

'What else did it do?' said Vallora.

'Who? What?'

'The Shydd. The one Harry said drew the poison from his body, like the one who did the same for Kat. What else did it do to him?'

They'd stayed with Harry until Mopper was fully recovered. Now they were following his directions to Rushymede, a coastal fishing town, where they could spend the night. He'd told them that the Deerwater flowed into the sea west of the town. If they followed the course of the river inland, it would take them through The Greenwood, all the way to Bowsprit.

Mopper was ahead. She gestured them on with a smile and clambered through the last of the trees. Hidden in the branches of one, a creature squatted. It watched Mopper from yellow eyes.

'You keep askin' me about Kat, and about Harry, or whoever he is now. *I* don't know. I'm no good at that sort of stuff.'

'But that's exactly it—*whoever he is now*. He's not the same Harry we knew back at Old Hall. You saw it yourself. Something's happened to him.'

'Yeah. A helluva lot. We know that.'

Vallora shook her head. 'He doesn't remember us, does he? Don't you think that's odd?'

'I told you, I don't do all that head-scratchin'. Ask Kat,' Dogpole said irritably. 'She's good at feelin's and talkin' to people, an' that. She's—'

'Sympathetic? Yes. I know.'

Mopper was calling them. They picked up the pace and broke through the trees. They were on a cliff of coarse grass. Mopper pointed to a sandy path leading down to a cluster of houses.

'The sea! And Rushymede!'

Beneath them, waves frothed gently against the a harbour wall. Vallora felt the familiar lurch of nausea.

***

Two fishing boats bobbed towards the beach. One drew in to the jetty. A fisherman in thigh-high boots jumped into the water holding a rope, and dragged the boat alongside. Two others hauled on a net of fish.

Vallora and Mopper were sitting outside The Hook and Basket, where they'd spent the night. Vallora's stomach pitched about uncomfortably. She hadn't joined her friends when they'd shared a dish of mussels the night before. She'd hardly managed to keep down a crust of bread. She turned her eyes away from the quay, where the fishermen were filling barrels with their catch.

Dogpole strolled out of the inn in his shirt-sleeves. They'd owed more than the silver piece he'd had in his pocket. He'd joked and flirted with the landlady until she'd agreed to give them rooms for the night. He'd spent the morning unloading barrels and stacking them in the cellar, to make up for the shortfall.

'That's it,' he said. 'No more nights at inns, and we've still got a long way to go.'

'It'll be OK. We can play it by ear.' Mopper grinned at Vallora. 'We're good at that, aren't we?'

Vallora gave a reluctant smile.

Mopper turned to Dogpole. 'I thought at least *you'd* cheer up, once we left the forest.' A drop of water splashed onto her upturned face.

'Gods, does it never stop rainin'?' he said.

'They call these parts the Wetlands. Take a wild guess.'

Vallora turned her back on the churning waves with relief. They climbed up the path. As they followed it along the cliff, they could look down on fishing villages, some no more than a row of three or four cottages.

There were stretches of sand with caves where the sea had eaten away at the cliffs, leaving fingers of harder rock sticking out of the water. After a few miles the path veered away from the coast and moved inland. The ground was spongy and flat. Wind blew off the sea, and crests of foam now tipped the waves rushing in. The cliff edge was soft, badly eroded. Out at sea, gulls drifted over a yellow sandbank, and settled, squabbling.

The land was marsh, stitched together with drainage ditches. In the distance, a white-painted windmill slowly turned its sails, and a group of men and women were cutting peat pits. Streams ran through the fenland, obscured by shoulder-high grasses growing either side. They had to pick their way carefully—in places the banks they walked on crumbled into the water.

Dogpole flung out an arm in warning. The tip of a staff protruded from reeds with feathery spikes. When they parted the canes, they saw a woman poling a raft along a river.

Further along, a narrow wooden platform had been thrown across the water. Beyond, they could see the roofs of roundhouses. Smoke found its way through their thatches.

The bridge was made from split trunks sunk into the riverbed. A few planks were fixed across with rope, leaving large gaps. The wood must have been brought there, as they'd seen few trees. They crossed the swaying bridge and squelched on towards the houses.

A man was coming from the opposite direction carrying bundles of cut reeds and a short-handled scythe. He was making faster progress than they were. Strapped to his feet were oval-shaped constructions like flat baskets. They helped to stop him sinking into the soggy ground. Mopper thought they were like the shoes her father had worn, the winter Keppelburg had been cut off by snow.

The inhabitants had built their houses on a raised area of firm ground. It was like an island rising above the marshy levels. There were eight or

140

ten dwellings, each with a patch of garden for vegetables. Some storage barns were raised off the ground on stilts, and an area was set aside for beehives. The houses were all built in the same way—roughly round, with sloping roofs of thatch and an entrance facing south-east. It looked like a prosperous little community. Outside the nearest house, an old man sat weaving baskets.

Children running about outside stopped to stare at the strangers, and the tallest boy ran past the old man into the house, calling for his father. He came out again with a bearded man, who looked them over. They were soaked through to their boots, bedraggled travellers, inexperienced in the fens, probably lost, certainly hungry. He invited them into the house.

The room inside was divided up, a loom and a bench for repairing tools nearest the door to get the best light, the central fire for cooking and eating, and, furthest from the door, the sleeping area. Daub walls kept out the wind, but the peat fire made it smoky.

The man's wife was baking a whole salmon inside a clay pot. A pan of vegetables was simmering. On a griddle were cakes. The smell made their mouths water.

'Come and sit. We don't see many travellers.'

Four children ran in, including the boy who'd announced their arrival. They smiled shyly at the visitors before joining them at the fire. The old man they'd seen weaving rushes came in silently. 'My father,' said the woman. They nodded a greeting and then turned back to the cakes. Their hosts exchanged a smile.

'How far have you come?'

'Rushymede,' said Vallora.

'A fair way. I won't pester you with questions 'til you've eaten.'

They were offered boiled vegetables and chunks of baked salmon which fell easily off the bone and was sweet to the taste. And then, as they began to dry out, there were plates of hot, buttered cakes. The children stared at the number Dogpole wolfed down. He winked at them, his mouth full, and they giggled.

He wiped his buttery chin and turned to their mother with an engaging grin. 'This is the warmest welcome we've had for many a day, ma'am, and these are the best cakes in Seywarde!'

The woman protested and blushed with pleasure. Her husband narrowed his eyes at Dogpole. Mopper made a choking sound and Vallora hid a smile. Dogpole could charm when it suited him, although he only seemed to exert himself at the prospect of food. But the woman seemed as taken with him as the landlady at Rushymede had been.

In any case, his appreciation prompted her to offer them shelter for the night. She said it was treacherous for people unfamiliar with The Levels to cross them in the failing light. The travellers, drowsy from the warmth of the fire, accepted her hospitality gratefully.

*** 

Next morning, Vallora and Dogpole made short work of cutting reeds. Their hands and arms were scratched but they were in good humour. It was good to be able to repay these hospitable folk, and both were happiest when they were outdoors. It was a relief to stretch their limbs. Inside the roundhouse, where every inch had a clearly defined purpose, they had felt clumsy, too big for the restricted space.

Under instructions from their host, they spread out the reeds to dry, then cleaned off the scythes, and sat outside sharpening the blades while they waited for Mopper. Earlier, two of the children had taken her to see a nest of dormice sleeping in a broken pot their mother had thrown out. Then they'd seen her chatting to the silent old man who'd joined them for supper. She'd been asking him about various landmarks in the landscape, and her rapt attention had thawed him. They'd disappeared in the direction of the river.

Mopper now sat in a round, flat-bottomed boat watching him. He was in the water, setting the baskets he'd made. They were tube-like; one end had a hole, the other was closed.

He said, 'There's eels sleepin' in that there mud.'

'Are there?' Mopper looked down through the murky water. 'I won't wake them if you don't.'

He grinned, revealing three good teeth and a lot of gum. "Tis late in the year. They should be gone by now, but the seasons is topsy-turvy, so us might be lucky.'

He moved upstream to check the traps he'd set the previous day. He lifted a couple and then pushed them back amongst the reeds. He grunted when the fourth was heavy. When the basket was cut, a brownish, snake-like creature thrashed about in the bottom of the boat.

Mopper scrambled away in disgust. 'What in all seven hells is that?'

'That be an eel, my duck. See, he swims in, but he can't turn round and swim out again.'

'Nearly put my foot on it. It looks poisonous.'

'Yerp. Blood is.'

He got into the boat, squatted down for a moment, and the eel stopped wriggling.

'What are you going to do with it?'

'That be dinner. Makes good eating, eel pie.'

Mopper pulled a face. 'I'll take your word for it!'

He grinned again.

'What now?' she said.

'Now you takes us back.'

He handed her the wooden pole and she dipped it into the water and made a few attempts to propel them forward. The boat began to spin. Seeing they were headed for the bank, she stabbed at the water.

The pole stuck. A water vole poked its head from the weeds and startled her. The boat rocked, water slopped over the sides and she let go of the pole.

'Oh no! What do we do now?'

'*I'm* goin' to sit 'ere and skin this eel. *You* is goin' to roll up your britches, and free my pole. And when you gets back in, learn to do a proper job.'

***

The landscape was open, windswept, and after the Withies, they felt exposed. They'd been given directions to the Deerwater, and followed a worn path, Mopper leading the way. Sometimes it took them across ditches, sometimes they walked beside a stream which disappeared, and they could hear water bubbling underground. At other times they had to leave the path to skirt flooded areas and pick it up further on. In the distance were narrow ridges of higher ground with houses. On one was a circle of stones. The eelman had told Mopper it was a meeting-place.

The skyline was low. The place seemed all sky. The only movement was from a marsh harrier on the prowl. It spooked a flock of lapwing on a stretch of water, and there was a sudden rustling as they rose into a spiral, showing their white bellies. Otherwise, the landscape was silent and brooding. Their eyes were drawn to a line of barrows on the horizon. The eelman had said it was called The Island of the Dead, and that ancient chieftains slept there.

Their hosts had given them food for the journey and suggested they rested at an outcrop known locally as Ceodor Murlynn. They would be able to shelter there, if necessary. 'If?' Dogpole had grunted, looking at the sky. Rain was never far away.

Ceodor Murlynn was easily spotted. It was a rock rising out of the turf, with a humped tree growing on it. Mopper left the track and climbed up to a shelf worn smooth by weather and travellers. She sat down, tucking herself against a slab of chalk at her back, and unwrapped the cloth. She looked squeamish when she saw the pastry.

'Eel pie, anyone? I saw the thing alive.' She picked up a rye bread roll filled with salted fish. 'I reckon we've had mussels, salmon, and perch. Nothing but fish. We've had it grilled, stewed and baked. Do you dream of meat? I do.'

Dogpole broke off some pie, and joined Vallora. She was scouring the flatlands, looking north for the Greenwood.

'It'll be OK,' he said.

'You sound like Kat.'

'It will. We'll find him.'

'You were right, we should have gone by road. It's my fault. We've lost time. The gods know where Blaise is by now.'

'It ain't that bad. It's not your fault. Not all of it, at any rate.' He smiled, but she was frowning.

'Take a breath. You get panicky when you think everythin' is on your shoulders. It ain't, you know. There's three of us. You might—'

'Good grief. Are you using head-scratching on me? I thought you weren't into that stuff.'

'I'm not an idiot, either. You're feelin' down because of…you know, not eatin', an' that. You got to eat somethin'. This pie is good.'

They climbed up to sit with Mopper, and leaned back, looking at the distance they still had to cross.

Two men were heading in their direction from further west. They'd been fishing in Lower Pike, and carried baskets containing their catch. From a distance they'd seen three travellers on Ceodor Murlynn. They intended resting there themselves before covering the last mile to their village.

When they got nearer they looked up, ready to call out a greeting. But there was no-one on Ceodor Murlynn. They paused and swapped their baskets onto their other shoulders. In all the flat grassland, they were the only people moving. Clouds rolled overhead, and there was a luminous, eerie light in the sky which meant rain.

One of the men said, 'Weather's turning again.'

'Yerp. Reckon you're right. Best not stop,' said the other.

They gave the rock a wide berth and hurried away.

\*\*\*

'In and out the dusty bluebells…'

Cassie hummed to herself and shut the window. She picked up a snow globe, gave it a shake, and carried it to the table. White flakes rose and whirled inside the glass, and when it cleared, she looked down on a barren, frosty moorland. Three little bearded figures turned their faces up to her as her giant eye hovered through the fog and filthy air.

The crone had her arms tucked inside her shawl, and the housewife looked resigned. The girl stared sulkily into the middle distance. Over the smoking bonfire was a grill. Some cooking pots were filling up with rain.

'How now, you secret, black, and midnight hags!' Cassie said, in a rallying tone.

The girl rolled her eyes. 'Whatever. So we've got this fillet of fenny snake and eye of newt? And there's this, like, toe of frog, and stuff?'

The girl seemed to query the evidence of her own eyes. Cassie tried to be encouraging.

'Well done. Basic, but it's a start. I must admit, I was hoping for something more adventurous. How about tiger's chaudron? That always peps things up.'

Thunder rumbled across the darkening fell. The women shivering in the rain looked up at her sourly. It seemed unlikely that a chaudron of any description would pep them up.

The housewife said, 'Where are we going to get

tiger's chaudron at this time of night, Hecat?'

'You're Class A beldames, aren't you? Use your initiative! And it's Mistress Chance, if you don't mind.'

The crone wrapped her shawl tighter and stuck her chin out. The beard wobbled fiercely.

'Well, Miss Chance,' she said, 'we're on a blasted heath, 'scuse my language, it's past Stephanie's bedtime, I'm wet through to me underpants, no-one's turned up and we ain't got any initiative left.' She pulled at a loose piece of grey wool. 'I don't see the point of the false beards, neither.'

'They were supposed to give you an eldritch swagger.'

'I don't do swagger,' said the second woman crushingly. 'I've got four children at home. I do disillusioned and taken for granted.'

Cassie looked down at the dying fire. 'I think, all things considered, we should give up on the barbecue. In any case, your guest...(her eye swivelled to a distant battlefield) appears to be delayed. Which wasn't on the cards. Why don't you put everything into that big pot and make a stew instead? It'll keep till he arrives.'

'We *could* do that,' said the crone. 'We *could* 'ang around and get pneumonia. Or we could go 'ome, 'ave a nice soak, and go to bed wiv' a 'ot water-bottle, like sensible people.'

'Fiddlesticks! You can't postpone a propitious meeting because of bad weather! It's Hagerstrom in winter, what do you expect? It's as bleak in midsummer. With midges.'

The sisters bridled with loyalty to their desolate surroundings.

'I'll 'ave you know,' said the eldest, 'we've won Best Kept Crags four years runnin'. There's a plaque up in the village 'all. Wiv' gold letterin'. Anyways, we gotta go.' She nudged the others. 'The brinded cat hath mewed. Thrice.'

'The hedge-pig whined,' added the housewife.

'Paddock calls?' offered Stephanie.

Cassie looked at her sharply. 'Does he or doesn't he?'

The girl looked blank.

Cassie sighed. 'If we're not doing it now, when *shall* we four meet again?'

The sisters fidgeted and glanced at each other.

'Look, nothing personal, but we like to keep things in the family,' said the mother.

'Three's a coven, four's a crowd?' suggested Stephanie.

They stared up at Cassie mutinously.

'Without me? Let's see how that goes, you saucy, overbold, hellhags.'

'Same to you. Cheerio.'

Cassie let them go because she was vexed. According to the cards, the meeting should have taken place. She was wondering whether she'd interfered with the outcome simply by being there. Was it one of those metaphysical thingummies? Like the one where the philosopher put a cat in a box, and asked his friends to guess whether it would be alive if they looked inside?

Cassie tended to suppress memories but she couldn't help recalling *that* occasion. She was reminded of it all the time. She'd only meant to observe, but got cross listening to the philospher's theories, and had intervened by rescuing the cat and bringing it home with her. She didn't approve of people playing at metaphysics with animals.

The cat in question distracted her by wreathing round her ankles. No rest for the wicked.

'I come, Grimalkin.'

\*\*\*

A red world span round inside Vallora's head. Someone was hitting her on the back of the neck. She rolled onto her side and was sick.

When she regained consciousness, the drummer was still beating a rhythmn on her head and shoulders. There were yellow flashes behind her eyes. She groaned and buried her face on her arm. The sound echoed mockingly back at her. There were other sounds, voices badgering her. She wanted them to go away and leave her in peace.

Afterwards she opened her eyes on a grey world. Silver nets of light danced in front of her and made her stomach heave. She shut her eyes. When she dared to open them a fraction, hoping the world would have steadied itself, the wavering patterns were still there. She realised they were reflections of moving water on the roof of a tunnel.

She was lying on her back, and the opening above her was the fissure in the chalk slab through which she'd fallen. She sat up and felt the back of her head. It was sore and tender. She didn't think the skin was broken, but her head thudded and her shoulders ached. She was on a narrow bank of sandy gravel next to a river. Chunks of chalk had broken off from around the hole above.

She crawled over to splash water onto her face. It was clear and cold. She scooped some up and tasted it. It wasn't salty. She thought it must be one of the freshwater rivers that dived through the chalk and continued its passage to the sea underground. She drank thirstily and then leaned over to wash her face.

'Vallora!'

'Kat?'

'Up here!'

Vallora got to her feet, shielding her eyes against the light. Mopper's face hung over the hole.

'Are you all right?'

*'Am I all right?* I've fallen fifteen feet. It feels like I landed on my head. I passed out. I've wrenched my shoulders, and my head is splitting apart. What do *you* think?'

'She's all right,' came Dogpole's voice.

'I'm coming down,' called Mopper. 'Stay where

you are.' She disappeared from view.

'Where exactly do you think I'd go?'

No-one answered because a rapid conversation was going on overhead. A shower of grit warned Vallora to move away, and then Mopper appeared, feet first, dangling in space. She was hanging from the end of Dogpole's arm. Then his shoulders and upper body filled the space, and Mopper swung lower. He must have been lying full length on the shelf above.

'OK. I can jump from here,' called Mopper.

She let go and dropped into a crouch, sending up a spurt of sand. Her eyes sought Vallora. She stepped over and gave her a hug. Vallora winced and backed away, clutching her shoulder.

'She doesn't look too bad, apart from the squint,' reported Mopper.

'Good.' Dogpole's voice floated down and echoed off the walls. 'By the way, you weigh a ton. You've dislocated my shoulder.'

'Thanks. You're always so supportive.'

'I *was* supportin' you and you weigh a ton. You've dislocated—'

'Yes, all right, you're a real hoot, Dogpole.'

'What happened up there?' said Vallora. She sat down again on the sand. Her legs felt shaky. 'One minute I was sitting with you...'

'I think we must have shifted the chalk slab when we leaned back against it. Dogpole grabbed hold of me or I'd have fallen through, too. Perhaps we triggered the secret entrance.'

'Secret entrance? To what?'

'A smugglers' haunt.' But when Mopper's eyes grew accustomed to the dark, she looked disappointed. 'Oh. It's one of those underground rivers. I suppose it must run to the sea.'

'Yes. Look, I don't want to sound ungrateful, but I don't see the advantage of us both being trapped. How do we get out?'

'We didn't know how badly you were hurt. We called out, but you didn't answer and you were lying so still, we were worried that…Are you sure you're OK? You're very pale.'

'I feel sick. My head is pounding. You're pale too.'

While they'd been talking, light had disappeared from the hole in the roof. So had Dogpole.

Mopper, staring upwards, could hear scuffling and a sharp exclamation.

'What had you in mind, now you're down here?' said Vallora. 'What's the plan?'

She was beginning to suspect they hadn't made a plan, and somehow this was more frustrating than everything else.

They heard shouting from Dogpole and a thud which sent stones and soil rattling down. Vallora and Mopper shuffled back against the tunnel wall. The gap above them widened as a lump of chalk detached itself and dropped, splitting into pieces. It was followed by a tangle of legs and arms which fell against them and sent them sprawling.

The stunned silence was broken by a catching of breaths, groans, a string of expletives, and then a lilting voice.

'Thou art hurt, Beloved of Lorelai?'

There was a pungent smell. Mopper looked into golden eyes glittering from a mass of brown hair…

…His voice was soft, but echoed along the tunnel walls and sped out to sea. The waves tossed the words into the air like a song. And the goddess heard her name and turned…

\*\*\*

According to Dogpole, the creature had appeared out of nowhere and leaped on him. For his part, the Shydd had seen Mopper being forced into the earth, buried alive by the ugly brute who'd struck him in the Bone Cave. The resulting struggle sent them plunging down. Vallora was at the end of her tether. She sat against the wall of the tunnel and put her throbbing head in her hands.

Dogpole rounded on the Shydd who stood protectively at Mopper's side. 'Why have you followed us, toad?'

'It ith thee way. She ith bound to me, ath Harree ith bound to my lord.'

'Over my dead body, pal.'

'I am willing.'

'Go ahead! Have a fight! That'll be helpful,' said

Vallora. 'All you've done so far is make sure we're *all* stuck here. Can we concentrate on getting out?'

The Shydd bowed. 'Thee Daughter of Ombriel ith ath withe ath beau-thi-ful.'

'That's nice,' said Vallora icily. 'Have you got anything practical to offer?'

***

Oculus had a headache and his eyes were dry and sore. When you have three eyes and all of them are sore, that is an almighty headache.

His 'break' had been no holiday at all, but endless bickering. They'd become inward-looking, self-absorbed, petty. Admittedly, he thought, we could be petty. Being a god doesn't mean you're perfect. Being an adolescent god learning the trade means you're far from perfect. But we are becoming *only* petty. We are diminishing through inaction.

Umbra glided into the dressing room, her robes flying about her like dark wings. The crescent on her diadem threw piercing rays of silver light onto his face. Oculus blinked and turned away.

'Celestial Moon…,' he began.

'Where are your eyedrops?'

'I was on the point…'

'You haven't been taking them, have you? No wonder you can't see straight!'

'I've got a headache.'

'Blurred vision is what you've got, and you've

156

been trying to hide it. Stirring things up, changing the subject...yes, and making me feel guilty about the Aelythir! But you haven't been The All-Seeing, have you, not for ages? We all have to do the maintenance!' She pointed to her starry diadem. 'Do you think I enjoy endless tweaking? Sometimes I don't know whether I'm coming or going. But it comes with the job.'

Oculus sighed.

'I know,' she said more gently. 'Your gift is a terrible one to bear. But only you can bear it. You *are* The Optimus Maximus, after all.'

***

They did not understand the words which had so infuriated Dogpole, but it appeared the Shydd considered himself to be some sort of guardian, and had followed Mopper across the fens.

'I'm sorry you're in this pickle because of us, but at least I can thank you properly. I couldn't have gone on without you. I owe you so much.' Mopper smiled, but the Shydd's expression was unreadable. She thought he hadn't understood a word. She tried again, speaking slowly. 'What is your name? I'd like to know your name.'

He put a hand to his breast. 'Sui Lithwyn rai athar Ombriel.'

'That's a freakin' mouthful,' Dogpole muttered.

'Aiee! He will crunch?' The Shydd crouched back

in horror.

'No, no! He's not going to eat you!' said Mopper. 'He meant…he meant your name is very beautiful. Too beautiful for his clumsy tongue. That's what you meant, didn't you, Dogpole?'

He glanced at Vallora, who folded her arms and watched him stonily.

'Sure. Why not,' he said.

Vallora's expression remained flinty.

He gave the Shydd what he imagined was a conciliatory smile. The creature hissed and pressed closer to Mopper.

'What is your name in our language?' she said.

The Shydd wrinkled his brow. He said hesitantly, 'I am Thmall Radianth come from Evening Thtar.'

Dogpole gave a snort of laughter. '*Twinkle*?'

'What doth thee troll thay?'

'It…it is our word for…um...the glow in the night sky from a shining star.'

The Shydd considered. 'Again.'

Mopper looked warily at Dogpole. 'The glow in the night sky from a shining star.'

The Shydd nodded. 'Jutht. That ith I.'

'Twinkle it is, then,' said Dogpole.

***

The walls of the tunnel were slick and smooth and there were no handholds. Even if they managed to reach up to the gap above, they knew it was unstable, liable to crumble away. Dogpole offered to throw the Shydd through the hole in the tunnel roof, but Small Radiance hissed and backed away. In the failing light, they turned to the river as the only means of escape.

They dragged slowly upstream, knee-deep for Dogpole and Vallora, waist-high for Mopper. The current was pushing her back, so she was hanging on to Dogpole to stop overbalancing. The Shydd swam in front of them so that he wasn't overturned by the wash of waves their heavy progress made. In the darkness of the tunnel, his body shone with a fluorescent light.

The river was getting deeper, the current stronger. The Shydd pointed ahead. There was another area of sand and shingle. A flat-bottomed boat, similar to that of the eelman's, had been hauled up onto it. Mopper gave a hopeful cry, and scrambled out onto the sand.

Next to the boat were stacked some small barrels, a chest, and canvas sacks. Mopper made out a series of lines on the chalk wall. They looked like tally marks.

'A smuggler's cache, do you think?' she said.

Vallora, still nauseous, her headache aggravated by the echoing cave, was tetchy. 'What's this fascination with smugglers? They're just thieves. Mohavians loathe them.'

Dogpole prised open one of the kegs and the lid span onto the sand. There was a spicy, warm smell of spirits. He dipped his face into the barrel and emerged grinning.

'It ain't fish. And it ain't half bad.'

Small Radiance made a 'pthah!' of distaste. 'Not good!'

'Tastes good to me even if Twinkle don't fancy it. I could do with warmin' up. Anyone else?'

'So that's you sorted, is it?' said Vallora. Then she added grudgingly, 'I suppose we could rest up here. Maybe my head will have stopped aching by morning.'

'And maybe you'll be in a better mood. Let's hope,' muttered Mopper.

She picked up a pair of waders from the boat and turned her attention to the sacks. One was loosely tied with a length of rope. She lifted out a couple of blankets.

'They must use this place as a stop-over. Thank the gods for thieving smugglers, I say. There might be more dry stuff here.'

Dogpole had thrown off his dripping coat and was keeping himself warm with the contents of the barrel and a cigarette. Vallora peeled off her clothes, wrapped herself in one of the blankets and lay under a tarpaulin from the bottom of the boat. Mopper gathered a collection of the smugglers' cast-offs from the other sacks and tossed a pair of rubbery dungarees to Vallora and a heavy, toggled jacket to Dogpole. She stepped into a pair of baggy cotton trousers and wrapped the extra material about her middle. Then she tied the rope round her waist to hold them up.

She offered the Shydd an oily woollen sweater. He sniffed it, wrinkling his nose. She shrugged a smock over head and nodded encouragingly. He put the sweater on. They looked at one other, dressed in ill-fitting, grubby clothes. Suddenly she laughed, a heartwarming sound in the gloom. Small Radiance looked at her curiously. They began to exchange halting whispers.

'Why do you call me after a goddess?'

'Thy hair ith like Morning Thtar. We did not alwayth live in dark. We love thee light.'

As Dogpole drowsed off, he heard them talking. He admired Mopper's persistence in trying to communicate with the creature. And felt a pang of jealousy.

\*\*\*

The boat and its cargo made uneven progress up the river. Dogpole steadied it from behind, one hand planted protectively on a barrel. Mopper, the long sleeves of the fisherman's smock rolled up over her elbows, wielded a short, flat oar with more enthusiasm than skill. Small Radiance squatted on the prow like a faintly-shining bow light. So it was Vallora, forging ahead in waders, who saw that the tunnel abruptly ended. Thick stems of vines hung down into the water, a green camouflage disguising its entrance. Vallora looped back armfuls to let the boat pass through, like a stagehand opening curtains on a scene of light and colour.

'Oh, how beautiful!' exclaimed Mopper, cheered by the sudden brightness. The Shydd turned to her, his expression echoing her delight.

The river ran towards them between banks which gave tantalising glimpses of a wood lit by evening sunshine. Vallora took hold of the prow of the boat.

'Keep paddling or you'll slip back downstream. I'm sure this is the Greenwood. I think we must have been on the Deerwater all the time!'

The river slowed and widened, the banks sank, and they could see the forest stretching out. A muntjac deer raised its head from the water, velvet ears twitching. A bark of alarm sent it leaping away. There was snuffling from the undergrowth. A bird trilled out a territorial warning.

Dogpole shoved from the back, and he and Vallora hauled the boat up the bank. Mopper and the Shydd jumped out, and then all four of them dropped onto the turf. Dogpole fished out a cigarette. He flicked a match alight with his thumb, lit the cigarette, and took a long pull.

'Amazing!' said Vallora without enthusiasm. 'How come you kept those wretched things dry?'

'It's a gift.'

'Not for the rest of us.'

But, weary as she was from battling the river, her

spirits lifted. They'd bundled their discarded wet clothes in the bottom of the boat. They shook them out and draped them over branches or spread them on the grass to dry in the sunshine. Then, under Dogpole's direction, they rigged up an improvised shelter for the night with the tarpaulin. They used his rope to tie it from the branch of a beech tree to a giant sycamore. He was insistent that they cleared the ground beneath, so they rolled away a decaying trunk and some dead branches, and cleared the litter of leaves.

'There's evil little ticks under that lot, just waitin' for us to lie down so they can bite us.'

When they'd finished, Vallora stretched out on her back, her head cradled on her arms, and stared up into the sycamore. Some fat, golden leaves floated down to crown her head and she brushed them off. Gradually she felt the tension ebb from her muscles.

Mopper sat beside Small Radiance. She pointed to the pendant he wore on his breast. A hole near one edge was threaded with a thin strip of leather. It was hung with a flat pearly stone, roughly circular, with lines scratched on it. Mopper traced the pattern with a finger.

'What do the marks mean, Lithwyn?'

'It thay the Aelythir are. We are, and we remain. It ith…comfort.'

Their heads were close together as they inspected the stone, his dark curls tangling with her fair ones.

163

Vallora yawned and shifted onto her side. Lithwyn and Mopper looked up, their movements mirroring each other. They talked quietly.

Dogpole paced, ill at ease. He retrieved the barrel from the little boat, and took a long drink.

Later, as the warm sunset faded, Mopper curled up in the shelter, breathing in the faint scent from a drift of ragged clover. Small Radiance sat a short distance away leaning against an oak, one hand on its trunk. In the dappled light under its branches, he seemed to have taken on the colour of the bark and become part of the tree. As Mopper watched him, she felt in tune with the forest.

It was lively and vigorous, from the fruiting trees and late-blossoming plants to the lush grass, unlike the deathly suffocation of the Withies. But it wasn't without its hazards. While nuts and crab apples grew plump on the boughs, fragile seeds fought to root themselves in the earth. Animals were hunting and being hunted. The green bird tapping at a tree was snapping up insects. Under the clover, beetles engaged in life and death struggles.

'This isn't a bit like the Withies, is it?' Mopper said drowsily. 'It's sort of…bracing. Full of life, full of creatures going about their business.'

Dogpole looked across at Small Radiance and took another swig. 'What sort of creatures?'

But she'd fallen silent. He couldn't relax so far from a road. He drew on a cigarette and listened to the aggressive birdsong and a shriek from a thicket.

Lithwyn pressed his ear to the oak and listened to its slow thoughts. The seasons were skewed, it grumbled. Summer wasn't like the summers when it was a young shoot; it should be winter, but autumn still strode the forest…

It was difficult to concentrate over the noise the mortals made. They were clumsy, undeveloped creatures, aware of only half the world round them.

But the girl with hair like sunshine was different. She hadn't flinched from him, as most mortals did. She wasn't as closed as the others, and had taken his part in the face of their distrust. He feared his lord would discover that he had helped her, and punish them both.

Close by, the mortals slept. The daughter of Ombriel snored, a more vulnerable figure now, the lines of worry on her forehead smoothed in sleep. The giant lay in a drunken stupor. The Beloved of Lorelai smiled as she dreamed.

If he left now, and went far away, his lord might not see her. The sweater irritated his skin. He took it off and started through the forest, running silently on bare feet. The trees watched and whispered, and someone heard their whispers and froze in anger.

***

The road continued west until The Flowerpot Inn, where the driver with the nosebleed was replaced by an equally taciturn man, and the carriage turned south. One of the thatchers pointed out a field he called The Butts. There were some soldiers packing up, having spent the afternoon practising with longbows. They cat-called when they saw two of their fellows had been lumbered with escorting a carriage full of locals.

The journey had been pleasanter since their encounter with the highwaymen. The passengers had became friendly, bound by their common experience. But gradually they'd all left—the thatchers, and the mother and daughter, at a row of cottages, and then the student at Lower Fold farm. Now Blaise was travelling alone. It was colder without the warmth of the other passengers, and the empty carriage flung him about so that he had to brace himself with his feet.

But finally, from the mud-spattered window he saw the lights of a town, and knew they must be approaching Bowsprit. It was the only sizeable place he'd seen since Burlap. At its edges it was swallowed in darkness. That must be Greenwood Forest, he thought. Closer to, he saw the town was approached across a stone bridge over the loop of a river. He guessed it was the Deerwater, and his spirits rose. He pressed his nose to the glass…

…Dame Chance slotted the picture into a stand

166

and placed it on the outer region of the gameboard. The figure representing the boy had no weapons and carried only the obligatory bag of gold.

She rolled a one. She thought that was fair; he hadn't travelled far from the city. Fields. Draw a card. Cassie reached for the pack, knowing she would turn up bandits—and then saw that two cards had appeared on the square.

A booming voice shook the room.

**'YOU CAN'T DRAW IF THERE ARE CARDS THERE ALREADY. THAT'S CHEATING.'**

Grimalkin's fur stood up in spikes. He legged it to the kitchen dresser and dived underneath.

Cassie picked up the cards. Followers. Men-at-Arms.

'Someone's cheating, for sure,' she said.

**'JUST SO YOU KNOW, I'M PLAYING FOR ZERO CREEP SCORES.'**

'Of course you are. Do you know what I'm playing for?'…

…The two patrolmen were already on the bridge. The driver whistled and flicked the reins to turn his horses into position. Three men emerged from under the bridge and ran towards the carriage. Two caught hold of the horses to prevent them getting onto the bridge. The carriage came to a stop. A third man yanked open the door. He made a grab for Blaise, but Blaise was no lightweight and fought him off.

After his initial shock at the attack, Blaise was angry that having come this far he might be thwarted by this ruffian. He grew hot as rage took him. He could hear nothing, see nothing, but the leering face of the man struggling to pull him onto the ground. Blaise struck out. He heard the man's teeth break against his fist, saw his eyes roll up into his head, and watched him tumble backwards to the ground.

Blaise leaned on the carriage door, breathing hard. When his heart slowed, he was aware of sounds and movement. The drumming of hooves, shouts, thudding feet, metal striking metal, the grunts and blows of fighting, and cries of pain. Something fell against the carriage. Then silence.

The patrolmen appeared. One had a scratch on his chin, and their scuffed uniforms would have made the sergeant's eyebrows rise. But they were trained men, and had quickly overcome the undisciplined attack of the men lying in wait.

The soldier with the scratch held the driver, who must have been involved in the fighting. He was bleeding from his mouth and one of his eyes was closing under a bruise. The patrolman looked curiously at Blaise.

'Know him, do you?'

Blaise shook his head.

The officer let go of the driver, who fell to his knees. Blaise saw that his ankles were shackled.

'That whistle he gave at the bridge was the signal

for the rest of the gang to attack. They weren't expectin' us, though. He tried to hold the carriage back, but it didn't take us long to see what was goin' on. You sure you don't know him?'

Blaise looked again at the driver. 'I'm sure.'

The officer shrugged. 'You're the only passenger left. They was after you for somethin'.'

The other officer was examining the body on the ground. 'Neck's broke.' He indicated a weapon in the man's hand.

Blaise held onto the frame of the door, swaying.

'Hold on there, son!' The first soldier got into the carriage and pushed Blaise onto a bench. 'Head down between your knees. Now listen. You see his knife? He was going to kill you. Keep your head down! So we ain't goin' to cry over him, are we? We'd best get you to a warm billet. A decent meal will set you to rights. Lucky we were here.'…

…'*Lucky*? Fiddlesticks! Oculus is loading the dice.'

Cassie left the gameboard to give her attention to a tricky manoeuvre. She knelt on the floor and dangled a little hessian bag. It was filled with catnip. She tried to tempt a lizard out from under the dresser.

***

169

In the morning, they searched the place they'd last seen Small Radiance.

'He's gone,' said Vallora. It sounded as if she wasn't going to miss his company. She pointed to the pendant Mopper had found with the discarded sweater. 'Maybe he dropped it. Or left it for you.'

Mopper shot Dogpole an accusing glance. 'What did you say to him? Did you frighten him?'

He gave a ferocious grin. 'I bloody well 'ope so or I'm losin' me touch!' Then he added heavily, 'No, Kat, I didn't scare him away.'

'Why did he go, then?'

'How the hell should I know?'

'It doesn't matter,' said Vallora. 'It's not as if—'

Mopper broke in irritably. 'Of course it matters! I wouldn't have managed if he hadn't—'

'Oh, you'd *manage*!' said Dogpole. 'You'd manage fine without anyone. You'll just miss havin' someone fawnin' over you!'

Mopper turned away coldly.

'I know you're grateful to the Shydd,' said Vallora. 'I understand, but—'

'No you don't! Don't say you understand in that sugary voice! You couldn't possibly understand! And don't call him a Shydd, it's an insult! He's an Aelythir, and he got a name. But he's not important enough for you to remember it, is he?'

Vallora's jaw dropped. That's unfair, she thought. I treat everyone the same. Her conscience pricked her. With the same condescension? I've been barely civil to him...The truth was she couldn't forget Harry's haunted face. A Shydd had bitten him and he'd lost his memory. What else had he lost? The creatures seemed to her to have a malign influence.

Vallora saw Mopper's forlorn expression. She was hitting out because she missed the...what had she called him? 'I only meant I don't think the Aelythir would be any help finding Blaise. You didn't expect him to come all the way with us, did you?'

'I don't know!' said Mopper. 'I don't know what I expected. It's strange he'd go without a word, that's all. And don't say it, Dogpole!'

'What?'

'You were going to say he *is* strange!'

'Yeah? That's what you think I'd be sayin' about the annoyin' little tick? You got no idea!'

'Why do you always have to belittle him!'

Dogpole smirked at her choice of words. 'It don't need me to—'

'Oh, shut up!' She turned her back on them, and looked down at the pendant in her hand. Then she slipped it over her head and under her shirt. 'Neither of you understands!'

'No. I don't know anything about the Aelythir,' said Vallora. 'So I don't think there's much point in puzzling over what made him leave.'

Her unease about the Shydd grew at the strength of Mopper's reaction to his disappearance. She began to gather up their few possessions.

'We should go. Our uniforms are near enough

dry. We can leave what we borrowed in the boat.'

They set off, looking for an isolated cottage in the north near Bowsprit, which was all the lawyer had been able to tell them. To their right were fences marking farms in Fallowdale. The fertile valley was sandwiched between Withy Woods and the Greenwood. They'd intended taking advantage of the comforts those homesteads offered travellers, and it was tempting to seek food there now.

They took a break to share out some beechnuts, blackberries and rosehips. The apples they'd found, not fully ripe, were tart.

'I'd even eat eel pie right now.' Mopper had said little, and looked drained.

Perhaps we should get some proper rest and food, thought Vallora. We aren't in great shape. What if Blaise has been taken by the outlaws? What if we have to fight to release him?

She turned at a slight sound. Before she could get to her feet, a hood was forced over her head. She struggled, but was held down. There were muffled cries from the others. Hands on her shoulders and arms pushed her forward. Her heart sank. They'd escaped the thugs once. They wouldn't let them escape again.

***

'They're doing *what*?'

'Frying sausages in front of your temple.'

'*Why*?'

'I think they're under the impression that you'd like it,' said Bretth.

Volte flared ahead to the Chamber of Marvels to consult the Scrying-Glass. In Dom Rei, in front of the temple dedicated to the god of Fire, they saw a procession of little figures carrying platters of sausages, eggs and bacon. They were handed by three Red Fryers to a fourth, who stood holding a shallow pan over the flames of a fire. As the smoke of cooking rose skywards and the worshippers chanted, priests in ceremonial aprons emerged from the temple, gathered the offerings onto silver trays, and progressed with dignity into the inner sanctum, to deliver them at the feet of the statue of Volte.

'I don't get it,' said the bewildered god.

'True on every level. Wanna see who does?'

The ritual was concluding. The Fryers, arms aloft, pronounced some final words. Then, as the fire died down and the worshippers left, they hastened inside the temple and bolted the doors. In front of an enormous wooden statue, the men in aprons were distributing a substantial fry-up.

'You've got to admit they've done you proud. It looks tasty,' said Bretth. 'They're really enjoying it.'

'I can see that, thanks. I can't even smell it!'

'No, well, the glass doesn't have smells.'

'I could fix it so it does.'

'I'd rather you didn't. I know what a crowd of mortals smells like.'

Volte watched jealously as the priests wolfed down crispy bacon. And then his attention was caught by the garishly painted statue. He goggled.

'Eldorath! Is that supposed to be me? It's hideous! What's that stuff comin' out of its mouth?'

'Flames? Putting an optimistic slant on it, it's most likely to be flames, wouldn't you say?'

'But they've got it comin' out of my—I haven't got flames comin' out of my…' He leaned closer to the glass and stiffened. 'It's a tail. They've given me a tail. And claws. With blood on.'

'It could be ketchup. They seem to like ketchup.'

'That thing is nothin' like me! It's a monster!'

'To be fair, they haven't seen you in a while.'

'Right. Dam' right!' said Volte, straightening up. 'And whose fault is that! This is all down to Oculus and his blasted Retreat! It messes with their minds, makes 'em imagine all sorts of…'

He paused, thinking. Then, alight with righteous wrath, he crackled through the halls leaving sparks in his wake. Bretth puffed along, encouraging one or two small fires on the way.

\*\*\*

In the snow globe, the sisters were lit by the flames of a burning castle.

'I don't understand how you could have picked the wrong man!' said Cassie.

I wasn't there, she thought. I didn't interfere. I didn't even *watch* this time. She shrank in horror at the bloody battlefield strewn with corpses.

'This is what happens when you insist on going it alone! Put it right! Start by giving the milksop prince an iron backbone!'

Her eyeball rolled over the three little figures, who had gone into a hugger-mugger at her words.

'I am speaking *metaphorically*,' Cassie said spikily. 'You use metaphors all the time, don't you? It's not that difficult. And what was difficult about spotting the right man?'

'Easier said than done.' The crone looked up at her defensively. 'You couldn't tell one from t'other. There was a hurly-burly goin' on. It were pitch black, and they was covered in blood.'

'And they wore little skirts that showed a lot of leg.' The married one blushed. 'It was distracting.'

'Distracting? You should have been focused on the job. You should have sensed something wasn't right. Was there no pricking of the thumbs? Didn't you at least have an *inkling*?'

'Didn't think we'd need one. Left it at 'ome with the broomsticks.'

'Don't get saucy with me! There must have been *someone* there without inner demons. Preferably with

175

a houseful of children to keep him occupied and stop him brooding. As it is, you've made the worst possible choice and I don't need a crystal ball to see this is all going to end in tears…*What*?'

She turned crossly at a disturbance outside her room.

'Ah. About time, too.' She threw a tea-cloth over the crystal ball. 'Open, locks, whoever knocks.'

Dust rose as the door shuddered. Heavy chains rattled and broke free. Bolts ground open. The rusty iron hinges screeched like protesting ghosts. The latch fell with a dull, heavy clang, the sound made when a ring of power is dropped onto a stone floor. From somewhere came the mournful hoot of an owl and the flutter of bats' wings. The door seldom had the chance to open, so was making a bit of a meal of it.

The god lowered his massive shoulders to peer through the doorway, where cobwebs hung like party bunting. By bending his knees and edging in sideways, he managed to shuffle to the centre of the room. The centre of rooms was his natural position. It was also where the ceiling rose up to a point, and where he could almost stand upright.

There was an affronted squawk. The god stared down and shifted a toe. 'Sorry. Didn't see you.'

He bent down to stroke the cat, but Grimalkin backed away. He stalked off, tail waving, to seek refuge under the table, from which position he watched the god with an expression of disapproval.

Oculus looked back at the precipitous staircase, with its unexpected twists and deceptive treads.

'That was...invigorating.' He rubbed a bruised shin. 'Tell me, Thou Unknown Power—'

'You don't need to be so formal. Granny will do.'

'*Granny*?'

'It's cosier,' said Cassie defiantly. 'Sit down, you're giving me a crick in the neck. Now, why are you playing at silly beggars?'

'I don't know what you mean.'

'Fiddlesticks! And don't pull that face. I've never known anyone who could sulk for so long and with such determination as you! But it won't wash. I know divine intervention when I see it.'

'And *I* know you're deliberately throwing traps in his way.'

'A*ha*! Admit it. You've gone out of your way to favour that boy. Why?'

'I haven't come here to be questioned. I'm The Optimus Maximus.'

'You don't seem to be enjoying it much.'

'In any case, how do you know?'

'Because every time I put a hiccup in his path, you come storming in and wrench the dimensions apart.'

'If you knew, why did you—'

'I wanted you to admit that you care about them. Some more than others, apparently, but to find a mortal you're fond of, for whatever reason, is a comfort. You should celebrate it, not try to hide it.'

'What do you mean, *for whatever reason*?'

'I know about showers of gold and such, Oculus. I wasn't born yesterday. Gods have always had favourites and favourite places. It's pointless trying to pretend otherwise. You've been too hard on the others. Give them a break.'

'A break?' said the god, with a hollow laugh. 'I *gave* them a holiday! They're just quarrelling.'

'I mean go easy on them, I don't mean an actual *holiday*! Gods don't have time off! Holidays are what mortals have. Holidays are when you should all be out and about cheering them up. I'm not surprised there's friction. How long has this been going on?'

Oculus mumbled something.

Cassie was shocked. '*How* long? Oh my days! That's an almighty sulk.'

'It's…everything was getting on top of me…it felt as if no-one understood…'

'Oh, I know that feeling. You've got a touch of the blue megrims. Get a cat.'

'*What?*'

'They're very soothing to have around, and even when they turn into lizards, it takes your mind off things. Get a cat. Or perhaps it's time you and Umbra thought about…How *is* Umbra?'

'Fine. She's fine. Everything's fine.'

'You've upset her, haven't you! I know she's prone to melancholy and cries at the least thing, but she adores you.'

178

'Does she?'

'Of course she does!' She looked at him sharply. 'You aren't on the ball at all! I suspected as much. Are you taking your eyedrops?'

Oculus squirmed evasively. 'I came to tell you …to ask you to leave the boy alone. Anyway, it's been…interesting. Thanks for the chat.'

'You're welcome. My door is always open.'

Oculus stared at her.

'No it isn't. It's locked up as tight as a gnat's…it's impossible to get into. You live in a fortress and the stairs try to kill you.'

'I was speaking metaphorically. In any case, you know the way now. It'll be easier next time.'

'There won't be a next time.'

'Don't be childish, Oculus. I've read the cards.'

***

Sessile had been listening with more attention to the Sounding-Board, and had received another lengthy, and critical, update from 'little Hildy', the elderly Patroness of the Sanctuary.

Oculus was looking with a pained expression at the walls of the Thrones' Room. Now he was back on the eyedrops, he thought magnolia had been a wishy-washy choice. He didn't like admitting it because he remembered it had been his idea. He was remembering a lot of things, and only half listening to Sessile's complaint against The Little

179

Sisters of Justice. He hadn't been in touch with his devotees for…ages, in fact.

'They've taken against the Wise Women?' said Oculus. 'They don't do much harm. On the whole. I remember one of them, a long time ago…a girl with freckles…' His eye on the past cranked into life and brought an image into view, a girl's bright, eager face as she held out a phial. 'She gave me a flower remedy. For depression and anxiety, she said. Just gave me wind…'

'Herbalists,' said Sessile severely, 'are the salt of the earth. They show a proper respect for plants.'

'As I said, an admirable group of women,' said Oculus hastily.

'But your Little Sisters call them witches. And if a girl has freckles, they say it's a sign she's in league with the Netherworld. They throw her in a river and wait for her to sink.'

'Sounds a little severe for flower remedies. And I like freckles. But if the girl is innocent…'

'They say she's innocent when she *drowns*!'

A tear glittered on Sessile's impassive cheek.

'Oh. And if she survives?'

'The Sisters say she must be using magic, and they set fire to her.'

'I see, so she's…'

'She's stuck between a rock and…another rock. They bring deckchairs, Oculus.'

'What?'

'They bring deckchairs to the fire. And picnics.

To make a day of it.' Sessile swallowed. 'It doesn't take a day.'

Oculus flexed his fingers. His palms itched. He imagined a girl with freckles being tied to a stake. And then he imagined his hand curling round a lightning bolt. He wanted to step on an island and drown it, and kick a mountain range to pebbles. He breathed in and out slowly and stared at the wall.

Come to think of it, he thought, I was the one who suggested we call the palace The Retreat. Which is as insipid as the magnolia, in name and concept. The gods in retreat? It wasn't an inspiring thought.

And the result? Aquaphraya, who couldn't be still for long, complained of boredom, and took off. Umbra and Lorelai were at logger-heads. Volte, usually the most cheerful of fellows, was prickly and bad-tempered. Bretth spent all his energy trying to wind him up. And stolid Sessile had become this drooping, sorrowful creature. Any minute now she'd say 'It's not fair'. As if being a god had anything to do with fairness! It sounded as anaemic as the magnolia. Divine Retribution was what they should be about. That had a suitably god-like ring to it.

'It isn't fair!' said Sessile.

My word, thought Oculus, I'm that good! Power surged through him like electricity. He glanced towards the doors of the Thrones' Room and they swung open obediently.

Volte roared in like a fireball. Bretth gusted in behind, but ran out of steam when he saw that the doors were still standing and hadn't been reduced to piles of ash.

'I *am* the All-Seeing, Bretth,' said the Three-Eyed god. 'Having fun is all very well, but please don't encourage Volte to burn the place about our ears.'

'You've seen what they're doin' in the temples?' raged Volte. 'All I'm sayin' is, if they *want* a fire-breathin' monster from the Netherworld, that's what they'll get! With bells on!'

\*\*\*

The gods scurried to the Chamber of Marvels. They carried the Sounding-Board and the Scrying-Glass to an anteroom, and gathered round for an overdue catch-up on Seywarde.

There were many temples celebrating the Water goddess in Westerburgen, a country which had a particular fondness for her. But her cult extended to Nordstrum, where a waterfall tumbling from a peak in Grittas Teeth was called Freya's Staircase.

Below, at Norvik, was a temple to the goddess covered in blue john. The mineral was found in Blodon Cavern, and only the  miners knew where to find the seam. But from the waterfall ran the Norwash, and its ice-cold waters were stained blue.

The mineral decorating the walls of the temple

had bands of purple, blue and golden yellow, which glistened in the frosty air. Inside there was a statue of the goddess carved out of rock crystal. She sat at a pool filled with water from a natural hot spring. The priests and priestesses bathed there every day.

The statue had been created with the same care and artistry as the outer walls. Aquaphraya was depicted as a girl with softly-waving hair strewn with pearls to represent drops of water. Her face was laughing as she enjoyed the pool. In all these details, the statue resembled the goddess as she had chosen to appear to Dogpole.

The sculptor had given her a long, clinging robe, and he had cut the stone at angles so that the different planes resembled scales. They glowed with a silvery sheen in the light from the pool. She sat paddling in the water. Below her knees, she dabbled her...

The gods craned forward over the glass.

'Well I'm blowed!' said Bretth.

'It can't be.' Sessile sat back. 'I think it's the way the water refracts the light.'

'Take it from me, light would need to do some serious refracting to get that effect,' said Lorelai.

'It's a tail, isn't it,' said Aquaphraya flatly. 'They've given me a fishtail.'

'See?' Volte said. 'Told you.'

Oculus was nonplussed. 'What is this obsession mortals have with tails?'

'The point is, they've started makin' up their own

stuff,' said Volte. 'And it's not only ugly statues.'

Wherever they looked on Seywarde, they saw bizarre new cults, fighting between temples, weird rituals. Perversions of the Three Rules. Punishments and killings, like those Sessile had described to Oculus. And all done in their names. What had been a break for the gods had been decades of their absence for mortals, who had filled the vacuum with half-remembered ideas and their own fantasies.

'The holiday is over,' said Oculus.

He led the way to the Thrones' Room. When he crossed the threshold, one eye glared at the walls.

'Let's get rid of this sickly colour. It's enough to quash any spark of inspiration.'

There was silence as the gods filed in. They were shocked at the effect of their withdrawal from Seywarde. But they were young and easily distracted. Oculus knew (his eye on the Present was in full working order) that uppermost in their minds was what colour the walls of the Thrones' Room should be. He saw them marshalling their thoughts for an argument. His eye on the Past recalled their quarrel over the holiday palace. His eye on the Future showed there'd be hard words and huffs, and it would take forever to agree.

Oculus glanced at the walls and with his thought they glowed gold. 'There! That's more cheerful isn't it!' he said. And he thought, I'll need all my eyes about me to keep them on track.

The Greenwood had once been a royal hunting ground, and was now home to deer, boar, and the dispossessed.

The forest was not only trees. As well as wooded areas, there were stretches of open heath, hills, rocky cliffs and deep valleys. Thickets of cobnuts and blackberries flourished there.

The Deerwater ran through the Greenwood from the Barrel Tops, fed by brooks and rills. It divided into streams to curl round The Tump, the flat-topped hill where sorrel grew. It loitered across watermeadows, where you could gather cress. It somersaulted over rocks to create waterfalls, investigated hollows, and spread lazily into pools. And then, as if recalling it had somewhere to go, it gathered itself together and dived underground to carve out a tunnel in a rush to the sea.

There had been heavy rains the previous year, followed by an icy winter and a spring slow in coming. But it was the rain, which had fallen relentlessly from July to September, that had done for the poorest smallholders in the river valleys. Floods had rotted their crops, and those who had cattle had to sell them when they couldn't feed them any more. And when they couldn't pay the rent, their homes were repossessed.

Some found work on local farms, but labour was cheap and they were paid a pittance. Some sought shelter in the Greenwood. They were used to training trees for hurdles, and collecting wood to repair their homes. They could coax vegetables from the rankest soil, and there was plenty to forage for.

The Greenwood had been a Royal Forest in name only since King Bardolph's death. There were no longer herders and verderers to patrol and manage it. So now you might come across houses of wattle and daub. This was against Forest Law, but who was there now to enforce it? The Marcher Lord didn't have the resources to rid the woods of bandits, let alone clear them of illegal dwellings.

One such home stood in Treegarth, a circle of oaks by a brook. A hunter came across it by chance. He'd been stalking a young boar and had loosed an arrow, but the wounded beast had charged off through the trees with a burst of speed he couldn't match. He smothered an oath, berating himself for his lack of skill. No meat for the hungry mouths at home, hours wasted, and a precious arrow lost.

He peered about, not recognising the place, and saw a boy cutting logs outside a cottage. He looked thirteen or fourteen, but large for his age, and he swung an axe through a tree trunk as if was cheese.

The youth glanced up and smiled, a smile of such benevolence and empathy that, despite his sour mood, the archer felt his mouth crease up in response. He stepped forward to speak, but a voice from the cottage called out the boy's name, and he laid down his axe and went inside.

The archer shrugged and turned back to find his own way home. He hoped he'd be luckier with the snares he'd laid, so he could at least take back some conies.

*** 

Vallora felt sudden warmth and smelled wood smoke. Hands pushed her onto a seat. She heard an agitated discussion, in which a female voice, quiet and authoritative, won the argument. Her wrists were freed and the hood was pulled off.

She looked round. She was sitting alongside her friends on a tree trunk. To one side of the clearing, a middle-aged woman was pouring water into a mossy dip in a boulder. Some men and women were cooking. Hanging over an open fire were cuts of venison. Surrounding the fire were more logs on which some old men sat chatting. Close by ran a beck, and across it ground had been cleared to grow vegetables. Vallora was puzzled. It didn't have the look of an outlaw encampment. She didn't think bandits dug the ground and grew leeks. It all looked too domestic. Beyond the clearing she made out the roofs of shacks hidden in the trees.

As soon as he was released, Dogpole reached for the nearest man and crushed him against his chest. In his free hand he held a menacing, long-bladed knife. Everyone stopped what they were doing.

187

The woman at the boulder made the gods' sign and hurried over.

'I'm sorry if you think we treated you roughly. The look-outs take precautions when they find strangers nearby. We've had to fight off raiders from the Withies, you see. Our existence here is precarious.' She paused. 'My name is Agatta. You're welcome to what we have. There's no hostility here unless you bring it yourself.'

Vallora whispered, 'Calm down for the gods' sakes, Dogpole! I've counted twenty of them, and six are armed.'

The tense scene was interrupted by honking, and two boys ran into the clearing, chasing some geese. A woman caught hold of the children. They became still, looking up into her face with alarm, and then turned to the stranger who held one of their group pinned against him.

'If they'd wanted to harm us, they'd have done so by now,' said Vallora. 'Let him go.'

He stood irresolute, rattled by the fearful looks the children cast in his direction. When he loosened his grip, the man shook him off angrily. The forest people continued to watch apprehensively until he sheathed the knife.

Vallora said, 'I'm going to talk to her. To Agatta. I think we're safe here because of her. Coming?'

Mopper followed. Dogpole stayed where he was. He was smarting from having been taken so easily, but he was also hungry, and had no wish to move

188

from the smell of roasting meat and the prospect of a meal.

The blackened pot on the fire contained a potage of leeks, parsnips, turnips, onions and barley. Dogpole watched one of the women lift a hot stone from the fire with pincers, dip it quickly into a bowl of water to wash off the ash, and then put it into the pot, which was soon simmering. She added some sprigs of rosemary and took another stone. The broth began to thicken and bubble.

A man was mixing oats, milk, and goose fat. He flattened sticky balls of the mixture between his hands, and put the cakes onto a flat stone in the fire to bake.

When Mopper and Vallora returned, Vallora said, 'They're all tenants and subsistence farmers. They lost everything in the floods. They've made homes for themselves here—'

'Outlaws!' said Dogpole.

'They're not bandits!' said Vallora. 'Look around you. They're just trying to survive. They thought we were one of the Marcher Lord's patrols, but Agatta told them we'd be armed and better dressed if we were.'

Everyone gathered round for bowls of potage eaten with rye bread, and then they had slices of meat cut from the roasting deer.

Dusk fell and it grew chilly. Most of the group drifted homewards, but some with dwellings close by lingered by the fire eating oatcakes and drinking

189

cider from clay pots. Agatta brought one of them across to Vallora and her friends. It was the man Dogpole had threatened earlier. Dogpole, with a bellyful of food, was willing to forgive the ropes and hood, and raised his mug in a good-humoured greeting. The man stared at him, unsmiling.

'Tyler can give you beds for the night. His wife and children have gone with her brother to visit family in Fallowdale.' She saw Vallora's guarded look and said, 'You can sleep by the fire if you prefer.'

Mopper hadn't spoken since they'd arrived at the camp. The warming effect of the food had worn off. She felt detached from the people round her. Their conversation was an inconsequential buzz. Strange images crowded her mind. She waved her hand in front of her face to brush them away.

Vallora noticed the peculiar gesture and was concerned. Mopper would normally have been the first to engage these strangers in conversation, but she seemed tired and withdrawn.

'We'll be happy to go with you, and grateful to spend the night under a roof,' said Vallora. Tyler gave a reticent nod. She turned to Agatta. 'You've been very kind. You've told us about yourselves but you haven't asked anything about us.'

'I expect you'll tell us when you're ready. As for kindness, you were hungry, and we understand that here.' Agatta smiled, her grave face creasing into lines of humour. 'Make sure Tyler gives you some of his cider. He's a terrible miser with it!'

Tyler grinned and relaxed. For the past half hour they'd all been enjoying his potent brew.

Inside a curtained alcove in Tyler's house was a straw pallet. Mopper sank onto it as if it was the softest down-filled mattress. She fell asleep at once.

Vallora sat on a settle by the fire, yawning over a cup of cider. Dogpole and Tyler were at the table, talking and drinking, their animosity forgotten. On entering, Dogpole had caught sight of a bow hanging by the door and had commented on its workmanship. Tyler had lifted it down and they'd pored over it. It was a finely-balaced piece. They'd discovered a mutual interest in weaponry. And strong drink. The barrel of cider by the table had taken a beating.

Tyler glanced thoughtfully at Dogpole's brawny arms. 'One thing we lack here is a blacksmith.'

'Best smith I knew was as skinny as Kat,' said Dogpole. 'But them wrists on those skinny arms! A fair wrestler, too. Quick…floored me once or twice.'

Tyler seemed to follow the argument. 'Very true. It's skill more than muscle. Still around is he?'

'She. An' it was a long time ago.'

Dogpole pushed his tumbler away. The drink had encouraged him to speak more freely than usual. He shifted on the chair, his brow furrowed.

Tyler interrupted his reverie. He was scraping a whetstone along his knife.

'This blade's got so thin, I reckon it'll snap if I

look at it too hard. I need a new knife. But like I say, we got no-one here can work metal.'

Dogpole smiled but shook his head.

'Can't blame me for tryin'. But I won't find a smith wanderin' the wood, they can find work anywhere. Mind, folk *do* turn up sometimes, like yourselves.'

He described coming across an old cottage, long empty but now re-occupied.

'And the lad there will have shoulders like yours when he's fully growed.' He replaced the knife in his belt and sighed. 'Lost an arrow that day.'

'What was he like, the boy at the cottage?'

'Big lad. Big smile. Hair the colour of straw.'

Dogpole was suddenly attentive. He went over to the settle, but Vallora had fallen asleep. The information would have to wait till morning. He took the cup from her slack hand and lifted her into a more comfortable position. Then he looked for somewhere to sleep himself.

\*\*\*

High above Dom Rei a firedrake circled, spouting flames. It had metal scales on its body, iron spikes ran the length of its tail, and its claws were tipped with red. It made a whirring sound as it spread its wings, and gave them a cautious flap, as if testing them for the first time.

The Guards had been called out, but they could do nothing to stem the pandemonium in the streets.

The terrified citizens shouldered them aside and trampled over each other to find shelter. A man paused in his headlong flight to scream at one of the guards.

'*Don't panic*? Are you nuts? That's a bedamned *dragon* up there!'

Captain Bell and his officers retreated to the flat roof of the Guardhouse, which gave them a view of the city. They watched the creature drift over buildings, spewing flames and setting roofs ablaze. It settled clumsily onto a nearby temple, its talons scraping on the lead tiles as it struggled to get a grip.

'Fire!'

Musket balls sped towards their mark. They pinged and clanged when they hit the dragon's scales. Its jaws opened wide, and fire scorched the terrace in front of the temple. There was a jingling sound as its tail thumped down, breaking through the roof timbers. It lashed at the walls until they were reduced to rubble.

The Guards clustered round the captain looked in horror at the devastation.

'Holy moly, that's the temple of Volte! You can get a damn good breakfast there!'

'Not today. The Fryers must have done summat to upset him.' Officer Lowlight made the gods' sign.

'It's a strange-looking dragon,' remarked another officer. She was woman of indeterminate years and extreme pallor.

'Familiar wiv' dragons are you, Velvet? I s'pose you're familiar wiv' all sorts of creatures from the Neverworld, ain't you?' said Officer Bloat.

'I wouldn't say I was *familiar,* no. Just a working knowledge. And that dragon is wearing a collar.'

The creature rose jerkily into the air and hovered in full view. Round its neck was a metal collar studded with bells. It crouched over the ruins, its expression one of intense concentration. It lifted its tail and extruded a torrent of thick, glutinous liquid which flowed out to form a sticky, viscous lake. Then, with a creaking of wings, the firedrake flew up into the sky, spraying the Guardhouse and the officers standing on the roof.

Captain Bell wiped a splash from his cheek, sniffed it, and gave a cautious lick. 'Ketchup?'...

...'Good effort, Volte!' said Oculus. 'The bells may detract from the overall menace, but it was a good start. What have the rest of you come up with?'

***

In Norvik, the priests and priestesses heard a booming sound from caverns deep underground. Aquaphraya's pool bubbled and foamed. A column of water shot into the air and thundered down onto the paved floor. The water roiled and overran the sides. The priests and priestesses fled.

The flood climbed higher, toppling the statue of

the goddess. The rock figure cracked and split, and was swept away. Icy waters rose up the walls and lapped at the pillars, searching out flaws in the stone…

And then Aquaphraya turned her attention to the rivers of Nordstrum, and with a word she froze the water in its tracks.

***

At Calico Bay in Mohavia, the Island of the Mariners, stands a stone temple dedicated to the god of the Winds. It's a simple, one-room structure facing the sea. The entrance has no door, and the windows have no glass, because the shrine is open to welcome the god, whether his mood is gentle or rough.

The eaves are hung with strings of shells and hollow pipes of horn, which herald the god's approach with music. Inside, hundreds of little trinkets swing from the rafters. They are carvings of boats and fish, made out of driftwood. Sailors work on them during voyages, and hang them up in thanks to Bretth for returning them safely to shore.

There are many temples celebrating the god of the Winds. At Traders Bay there is an upmarket version built of brick, with a bell-tower. It is hung with tributes made from silver or decorated with precious gems, given by traders grateful for the safe arrival of merchandise, or requesting the god's blessing when they sent ships to far-flung lands.

But The House of the Winds in Platt Obscura was reputed to be the most opulent of Bretth's temples. The island is east of Dom d'Or, the most easterly point of Seywarde. Sailors who ventured so far brought back tales of a sunny golden palazzo with tiled walls, shady colonnades, crystal fountains, and sunken, perfumed gardens.

They reported that the chief priest, the Great Ventilator, had scores of attendants, whose office was to bathe him in scented oils, feed him pomegranate seeds, and dress him in silken robes before carrying him about on a litter. They said the Ventilator was enormous in every way, enormously rich, enormously greedy, and just plain enormous.

There weren't any gifts to the god hanging in the shrine. The Great Ventilator had a treasury with chests of gold and silver pieces. He had a lucrative sideline selling a favourable wind to merchants visiting the island. And when Bretth saw this, he huffed, and he puffed, and he blew the House down.

*** 

A group of black-clad women were assembled like agitated ravens on the bank of the Deerwater. They were priestesses from the temple of The Little Sisters of Justice in Bowsprit. Their chief priestess,

196

the Hi-Hatt, was distinguished by her white, cone shaped cap of office and the ear-shredding volume of her voice. She was haranguing her audience in shrill tones. The cowed Sisters shrank away uttering frightened squawks. A grey-haired herbalist stood to one side with her fingers stuck in her ears.

When Fraya joined her, Sessile was watching the scene on the Scrying-Glass and her cheeks were flushed with indignation.

'They're accusing Sienna Podd of black magic!'

'Nonsense! The dear girl wouldn't harm a wood louse!' Aquaphraya smiled fondly at the little figure on the screen.

'You know she must be at least eighty, Fraya? Hardly a sapling any more.'

Aquaphraya beamed happily. 'She is to me. Lorelai says I see them through rose-tinted glasses.'

'Everything would be rose-tinted if Lorelai had her way! That man accusing Sienna is Gummer Brittle. She gave him her remedy for indigestion. She says she got it from her great, great, grandpa's recipe book, and claims *he* got it direct from me. Which is probably true, as it's infallible. And I used to get out more in those days.'

'We all did.'

'Now Gummer's got a cold, and he's blaming it on the medicine…'

Fraya interrupted. 'I'd like to listen in for myself if you don't mind. *Show*, don't tell.' She turned to the Sounding-Board. 'You've got it on mute! Why have you switched it off?'

Sessile turned on the volume. The strident tones of the Hi-Hatt were accompanied by a cacophony of twitters and clucks from the excitable Sisters.

Aquaphraya winced and stepped back. 'So that's what a murder of crows sounds like! Is that what they're planning?'

They tuned back in when the chief priestess appeared to be reaching her conclusion…

'The evil concoction was not efficacious?' yelled the Hi-Hatt at the top of her lungs.

'Dunno about that, but it cleared me guts out fine,' said the old gentleman. 'Only it's give me a shockin' cold.'

'Of course you've got a cold!' said the herbalist. 'Anybody your age would get a chill bathin' in the river of a mornin' in the altogether. The rest of us gets a nasty turn when we sees you, an' all!'

'I were all right 'till I took that medicine.' Gummer sniffed ostentatiously and wiped his nose on his sleeve.

'You were all right 'till I asked you to *pay* for it, you old skinflint!'

'See that?' said Gummer, pointing a trembling finger. 'She's givin' me the evil eye!'

The Hi-Hatt squawked and flapped her sleeves. The Sisters chorused 'Oculus defend us!' It wasn't clear whether they sought protection from Sienna or the high priestess.

'Mistress Podd has confessed her guilt!' cried the Hi-Hatt. 'She's put a spell on this poor man because he refused to pay for her black magic.Take her to the ducking stool! We've heard enough!'

…'*So have I,*' said Sessile grimly. She stretched a hand to the screen, and the branches of the trees by the river trembled, although no wind blew. The little figure of Sienna was lifted into the air and borne away to safety.

Branches broke off and spun upwards. There was a tearing sound, and the ground shook. The trees were ripping themselves from the earth.

The Sisters scattered, screaming, as stones and clumps of turf hurtled past, leaving behind deep pits like accusing mouths. Slowly, very slowly, the trees began to move, shambling forward on their roots. They reached out to catch the fleeing Sisters in twiggy fingers, and pressed them close, gripping and suffocating, as they carried them to the river.

The Deerwater leapt at Fraya's command. The waters rose, engulfing the trees and their helpless victims…

And Oculus stepped into the room. The scene on the Scrying-Glass froze.

'I can't let you destroy them. They're my followers and they made an appeal to me, however late in the day. You heard them.'

'Oculus, you can't do this!' said Sessile.

'I can, you know. I'm the one with the biggest hat. Metaphorically speaking, as Granny would say.'

Aquaphraya was incredulous. 'You're going to save them? After what they've inflicted on so many innocents? That's not…'

'No, it's not fair. It's got nothing to do with fairness. I call it Divine Retribution.'

The Scrying-Glass flickered back into life.

The branches holding the captives peeled away. The black figures of the Sisterhood clawed their way out and rose into the air screeching, their robes transformed into the tattered feathers of birds of prey. They had unblinking eyes and cruel beaks. The largest of them had a tuft of white plumage on its bald head. The monstrous birds wheeled about the treetops and flew off in different directions. Their raucous cries filled the air, like omens of impending disaster.

'I have sent them to sit…roost…on the gables of my temples for eternity. Their cries will be a warning against misusing power and calling it Justice.'

On which majestic note Oculus strode off, flexing some pretty powerful muscles. Metaphorically speaking.

'An eternity as one of those dreadful creatures!' said Aquaphraya. 'What a horrible fate! Oculus' idea of Divine Retribution is a frightening prospect!'

'Did you know he had a granny? That *is* a frightening prospect,' said Sessile.

The drowsy autumn had held winter back, but leaves had fallen in the night and the air was brittle with frost. Mopper had slept badly. She'd had nightmares about walls closing in on her. She shivered in the cold dawn as she washed her hands and face at the beck.

After a breakfast of porridge, Tyler took Vallora and the others to see Agatta. By now even Dogpole felt confident enough to trust them, and they asked for help in their search for Blaise. They recognised Blaise from Tyler's description, and he'd answered when the voice inside the cottage had called his name.

The archer said he could put them on track to the cottage, and they should reach it by late afternoon. Agatta found them serviceable clothes, warmer than those they'd been wearing, and they left better equipped than they'd arrived.

Tyler waved them off. 'Always a place here for a smith!'

'You don't give up easy, do you?' Dogpole called back.

'Nor should you. Good luck!' cried Tyler, with a wink.

A flush stained Dogpole's cheeks. He looked at Mopper but she was wrapped in her thoughts.

Vallora took a last look at the camp. She lifted a satchel of provisions onto her shoulder.

'They've got so little, but they're so generous with what they have,' she said earnestly.

Dogpole put on the heavy, fur lined coat Agatta had found for him. 'How generous have they been, an' how long before we can eat it?'

They made several stops on the way, more than Vallora would have liked. She took Dogpole aside.

'Something's wrong.'

Mopper lay against a backpack, her eyes closed.

'Probably her knee playin' up a bit.'

'You know it's not that! Her knee has been fine since the Shydd…since the Aelythir…Look, she likes leading the way, doesn't she? Now she's lagging behind.'

'She just needs summat to eat.' Dogpole brushed crumbs of cheese from his coat.

'For the gods' sakes, it's got nothing to do with *food*! Every time we stop she needs to rest longer. Look at her!'

'She looks all right to me.'

'She looks exhausted! Can't you see? Her cheeks are sunk, like…'

Mopper woke at Vallora's raised voice. 'Is it time to go already? Is everything all right?'

\*\*\*

It was dusk by the time they found Treegarth. The cottage was as Tyler had described it, but the place was deserted. No welcoming smoke rose from the chimney, and the windows were dark.

Dogpole lit a cigarette and sloped off, saying he'd do a recce. Mopper sank onto the doorstep. Vallora pushed open the door, with little hope there would be anyone inside.

There was one room, and stairs led to an attic bedroom. The hearth was a heap of ash. An embroidered cushion lay on the floor, and there were the remains of a meal on the table. She was aware of a lingering, musky smell. She recognised it at once, and it set her on edge. The cottage felt suddenly alien.

She said nothing when Dogpole came in. He already looked worried, and it wasn't only that they hadn't found Blaise. He'd seen Mopper's flagging steps, and now shared Vallora's concern. Mopper was listless and quiet. There didn't seem to be anything physically wrong with her, and they were at a loss to account for it.

Dogpole filled a pail from the well at the back of the cottage. He found some stubs of candles on a shelf and lit them. The soft light revealed a comfortable, well-equipped room. A cupboard decorated with stencilled flowers held butter, cheese and eggs. There were loaves inside a crock, and a larder with a basket of root vegetables. He began assembling a meal.

Vallora took her cue from Dogpole, and tried to bury her anxiety by concentrating on practical matters. She knelt by the remains of the fire and swept the ash into a heap. It was warm underneath, evidence, along with the well-stocked larder and half-eaten meal, that the place had been only recently abandoned. But it was a waste of energy wishing they'd got there sooner. She squatted to shovel the ash into a bucket, and built up the fire from a box of kindling and logs.

Mopper had trailed across to an armchair by the hearth. A patchwork quilt was folded on the seat. She gathered the quilt around her shoulders and sat down. When the fire took hold, flames danced in her eyes and made it difficult to focus. Everything around her was fading, and a different scene was edging itself into her mind. Sparks from the logs flew up to the beams like fireflies flitting though a forest. The walls of the cottage began to crumble into earth and sprout roots…

'We'll 'ave some supper, no time.'

The voice tugged her back into the room. A man knelt in front of her, balancing a pan on the fire. He looked up and grinned. His face was familiar.

'I'm not hungry. I think…I think I need to lie down.'

She stood up, holding the quilt around her, and Dogpole caught her as she fell.

\*\*\*

The underground chamber had earth walls. The prince sat in a chair formed by the roots of willow and hazel trees. His voice was bitter and accusing.

'Did you wish to stay away from me forever?'

'You banished me! You speak as if it was my choice!'

'It was. You left me to protect our people alone. Was it worth it, brother? Has it made you happy?'

Lines of grief deepened in Meredydd's face. He said quietly, 'Why have you brought me back?'

The prince abruptly stood.

'I did not banish your daughter. You tried to hide her from me. That was unkind. She is my blood.'

'She is the daughter of Elodie.'

'A mortal,' sneered Alfyndur. 'You turned your back on me to live amongst those who despise us! They are murderers, and their maggoty half-lives are loathsome to me! But Olwyn is all Aelythir, and you know it!'

Meredydd was silent.

'Do you wish your rootless existence on her?'

Meredydd said nothing.

'What will she do outside? She won't be safe. She belongs with her people.'

'Is that why I'm here, Alfyndur? You want my daughter?'

The prince grasped his brother by the shoulders.

'Our race does not thrive. We need children.'

'You won't take mine!'

'I already have. It's you who has been difficult

to find. You, and Olwyn's child. But you cannot hide forever. Olwyn tells me nothing, but you will persuade her. Where is the boy, Meredydd?'

\*\*\*

His massive frame shook the walls as he passed. Floors buckled under his mighty tread and his blazing gaze melted the silver statues. His hair streamed like molten gold. He was conscious of his divine power. And his smile was beautiful and terrible to behold.

He burst into Umbra's room and stood before her in all his glory.

'Good heavens, Oculus!' she faltered.

'**YES! THEY ARE *VERY* GOOD, MY LOVE!**'

'You are…magnificent!'

'**YES!**'

'Overwhelming, in fact!'

'**I AM!**'

'No, I mean it. I can't focus. Can you…turn yourself down a bit?'

Oculus reached out to take control of his power and dimmed from blindingly sublime to a megawatt of splendour which was just about bearable—if you were a goddess, and used to that sort of thing.

Umbra found she could breathe again. 'You're still scorching the furniture.'

Oculus concentrated. It was difficult trying *not* to be awesome when you'd accepted the fact that

206

you *were*. How had he managed it, back in the day when he'd taken human form? He checked to see if Umbra was still clutching the arms of her chair. She was smiling up at him with adoration in her starry eyes. He'd dwindled enough.

The Pantheon was summoned to the Thrones' Room. Oculus was pulling rank and doing some *summoning*, for the first time in decades. The gods looked up at his entrance with interest.

He exclaimed, 'Yes! I look different today, don't I!'

'Not really,' shrugged Bretth. 'What's this idea of yours?'

'You look fabulous, Oculus,' said Lorelai. 'Have you done something with your hair?'

Sessile said, 'You look exactly the same to me.'

'Only more so,' said Fraya.

Volte nodded. 'You, with bells on.'

'And your dressing gown,' mumured Umbra.

But on the instant, Oculus had clothed himself in golden armour, the sigil of the sun on his breastplate. A helmet branched with antlers clasped itself around his head.

Volte perked up. 'Are we going to war?'

Oculus smiled. 'It's a long time since we went on a hunt.'

The Wild Hunt had grown out of use. In essence it was the gods showing off, reminding mortals of their existence. They would gallop across the sky like a pack of huntsmen, accompanied by the noise of trumpets and baying hounds. They usually chose midwinter for this event, because the menacing cold and unrelenting darkness provided a suitably dramatic backdrop. In those days, the gods had been nothing if not theatrical.

People were scared witless at the sight of their gods riding across the night sky. It was said that the Wild Hunt presaged disaster, that men were abducted, dragged up into the frantic chase, and whisked away to the Netherworld. On the plus side, everyone appreciated the gods putting on a performance at the back end of the year. It showed they were thinking of them.

The Pantheon hadn't celebrated the hunt for a long time. They hadn't been at any of the festivals. Not the Harvest Home, Yule, or the moon festival, when people made paper lanterns and put candles inside and watched the wind send them floating into the sky. They hadn't attended the dragon boat race, or the midsummer festival when youngsters leaped across bonfires. Nor the spring celebration when two were chosen to be crowned Rob-in-the-Hood and Marion the Maid, and girls and boys plaited the ribbons of maypoles on village greens, and everyone went hog-wild when the gods themselves joined in the dance in the guise of Herne the Hunter, the Green Man, and white stags with silver horns…

Since they'd withdrawn into The Retreat, the gods hadn't put in an appearance at any of the holidays. But Oculus had come to terms with himself, and had decided it was time to reinstate those reminders of the Pantheon's existence.

'Suit up!' said Oculus Maximus.

*\*\*\**

The call to arms resulted in hurried visits to the Chamber of Marvels. Weapons and armour were unearthed and dusted off. And Lorelai, who had no interest in either, invited Umbra to breakfast.

Oculus had had a quiet word with the two goddesses. Delivered at a volume requiring capital letters in bold format. He was in mythical hero mode, blazing with charisma, and rigged out in shining armour with all the trimmings. It was the look run-of-the-mill champions aspired to. The goddesses were impressed.

He had made it clear that he wanted an end to their hostility. The Pantheon should be of one mind. By which he meant *his* mind. So Lorelai had felt obliged to send a syrupy invitation to Umbra, and Umbra had reluctantly left her daytime slumbers.

Lorelai's morning room was drenched in light. Primrose curtains fluttered at the open casement. Umbra appeared wraith-like in the sunshine. She shrank away, feeling at a disadvantage, which she suspected was Lorelai's intention.

'I'm sorry. I cast a mist to hide the Aelythir from harm,' said Umbra. 'It was not meant to insult you.'

'You trespassed on my territory. But you are a sister goddess.' Lorelai smiled sweetly. 'And I am known for my generosity and forgiving spirit. I accept your apology.'

Umbra stirred uncomfortably. The daybed on which she reclined concealed spiky springs, just as Lorelai's saccharine words hid barbs. There was an edgy silence.

'I do not wish anything to sour our renewed friendship, dearest Umbra, but...'

Umbra braced herself, wondering what further grievance Lorelai was fretting over.

'...but I thought you should know your prince has sunk his claws into a mortal. Perhaps he thinks no-one will care, because she is blonde, and blondes are of no account.'

She shook her hair. Umbra recognised the sign. She was irritated by the description of Alfyndur as 'your prince', but held herself in check.

'I don't understand.'

'The girl is named for me. By one of your own pet Aelythir, to my surprise. But I hear when one is named mine, Umbra, whoever does the naming. Be certain that I do!'

Knowing the name of a thing gives you power over it, but to give a name is even more powerful. A childish nickname sticks. A random phrase flung at school lasts a lifetime. It becomes an indelible part of who you are. 'Beloved of Lorelai'. Imagine the consequence of invoking the name of that goddess. A goddess notoriously jealous, quick to detect slights, and with an elephantine memory for harbouring a grudge.

'How does your prince dare to encroach on a mortal under my protection?' said Lorelai. 'Are you so besotted with him that you've granted him the power of a god?'

***

Grinding ores into powder and mixing them, subjecting them to fire, pouring the molten metal into moulds and then shaping it—magical alchemy! Volte particularly enjoyed the bit where he hit things with a hammer.

But at this moment his swarthy features, lit by the flames of the forge, were absorbed in a more delicate operation. He was making adjustments to the little automaton he called Torch. Though 'little' was a relative term. The firedrake was only small when compared to the colossal proportions of the gods, who could step on you and not notice. And occasionally did.

Volte smoothed out the blips in the mechanism of the wings, and inserted stronger springs into the tail section. He replaced the bellows which fed the fire-box with a cylinder, piston, and rods, which worked like a pump. He got creative with the eyes, fashioning bulbous, lamp-like projections which gave Torch a startled expression.

211

And then the god put his hand into the furnace and took a single spark between his finger and thumb. He placed the tiny pinch of life into the firedrake's mouth. Which had genuinely startled Torch.

Volte fed him charcoal, and oil so silky smooth Torch purred. He flew up to perch on the god's shoulder, hooking his talons into the links of Volte's shirt of mail. He snored contentedly, puffing out smoke rings.

Volte picked up his helmet and made a selection from the rack of tools in preparation for Oculus' inspection in the morning.

***

Umbra bent to the Scrying-Glass. Lithwyn lay in darkness, limbs twisted in agony, bound with strips of willow. His lips were drawn back in a voiceless scream, but Umbra heard it.

The old race was coming to an end, and Umbra had wept for the loss. But her protection had fed Alfyndur's arrogance. Confident of her support, he had become a tyrant to his people, and now laid claims on a mortal.

The curling mist parted and the goddess of the Night appeared in the guise of a warrior queen, an armoured figure of breathtaking beauty and dread.

'What is it you do here, Prince Alfyndur?'

'I look after my own, Evening Star.'

The scene in the Scrying-Glass appeared in front of him, like an image viewed in a bubble.

Alfyndur was undaunted. 'It is forbidden for the Aelythir to have dealings with mortals. They know they will be punished.'

'You have all but destroyed this little one because he showed pity.' The goddess shook her head and her eyes filled with tears. 'Ah, Alfyndur! You were not always so unbending. Are you sure you will never need pity yourself?'

But the prince had become too proud to accept rebuke or to heed her warning. 'I carry out the law of the Elders.'

'The Elders made no such law! I was there at the beginning, and I know this work is of your own devising.'

'Nevertheless, *I* am Lord of the Aelythir, Lady. It is *I* who governs here.'

Umbra showed him the image of a girl wrapped in paralysing dreams, like a butterfly trapped in a chrysalis.

He flinched, but said, 'There is a debt to pay for a healing.'

'A debt of gratitude, nothing more.'

'Do not school me! *I* will decide what to do with her!'

The goddess looked down on him and her eyes were cold as distant stars. 'You do not decide the fate of mortals, little lord! Even a god hesitates, and you are not a god. Do you think we sleep? You reach too high!'

Then Alfyndur was afraid and sank to his knees.

'Gracious Lady, I have depended on your tender support and trusted in your love—'

'Then you have deluded yourself. Am I not the Evening Star? It is foolish beyond measure to hazard everything on my constancy!'

The full moon rose until her shining presence topped the trees. The forest was flooded with light, and the goddess withdrew her protection from Withy Woods.

\*\*\*

Lorelai's shell-shaped chariot glided over the wine-dark sea. She stretched out her white arms. Rays of light streamed from the tips of her fingers and spread over Seywarde, bringing a new day. She looked down at her rose temple on the coast at Piersport. It faced east, and was one of the first to receive the beneficence of the dawn.

But there was no-one at the temple doors to witness her glorious arrival. No Seers to welcome her with cymbals and song. No perfumed oils burnt in celebration. No dancers to greet her. No flowers laid in thanks. What could be more important than according their goddess due reverence? What is the point of a stunning entrance if no-one is there to watch and applaud?

Lorelai pouted. Her whip brushed the flanks of

her horses. They churned the sea into foam as they rose towards Piersport and their burnished hooves grazed the harbour roofs.

Below, the Seers were in the streets questioning householders about their sleeping habits.

Lorelai loosed her robe and let it fall. The Seers, looking skywards, were struck dumb and blind, their eyes dazzled, and fell senseless to the ground. The chariot swept onwards, and the empty shrine of the goddess collapsed in on itself like crushed eggshell.

And from that day, the Seers of Piersport were a silent order, dim-sighted, and homeless. For the goddess had revealed herself in all her divine beauty, and the sight was too much for a mortal mind to comprehend.

\*\*\*

The Pantheon was assembled before the central pillars of the pink palace. The alabaster pavement sparkled.

Oculus looked on with satisfaction. His golden chariot was pulled by an aurochs with curving horns. Its shaggy coat steamed in the dawn light.

Umbra's black stags pawed the pavement, as if too proud to set their hooves on the ground. Aquaphraya's hippocampus flared its nostrils and blew bubbles, coiling and uncoiling its scaly tail. Sessile's tusked boar snorted and stamped. Bretth, a bow at his back, sat astride a mighty hovering falcon. Volte drove a chariot with go-faster stripes. He wrestled the reins of a winged gryphon, which twisted its head round, trying to nip the other animals with its beak.

The gods, as anxious to impress one another as their mounts, examined each other's equipment.

Bretth looked over Volte's stack of weapons.

'Cool flame-throwers.'

'Thanks.' Volte eyed Bretth's winged helmet. 'Nice feathers.'

The firedrake clinging to his shoulder span its eyes.

Finally, Lorelai joined them, descending from the clouds in a chariot drawn by four sleek horses. The delicate folds of her gown floated behind like trails of gossamer, and her hair lifted in curling strands of palest gold. She was a little out of breath, her lips parted, her skin aglow with the soft colours of sunrise. She leaped down on bare feet and peeped up at the assembled gods from under blue eyelids, well satisfied with the effect of her entrance.

'Good of you to join us. Are we early?' said Umbra acidly.

Lorelai's voice dripped honey. 'I've been bringing dawn to Seywarde, from forest to mountain, valley to desert, and to every island. I don't know what the rest of you call early.' She turned to Oculus and smiled. 'You look divine.'

'Er, yes. Well, now we're all here, we can make

plans for the witching hour, as Granny would say.'

As the gods made their way inside, he caught up with Umbra and whispered, 'I must say, I find that very disappointing. She isn't entering into the spirit of the thing at all. She's hardly wearing anything…in the way of arms, I mean.'

'On the contary,' said his wife. 'Lorelai's weapons are devastating.'

\*\*\*

The rivers of Nordstrum were frozen glaciers. The ice on Skarlake was three feet thick. Codger Huddersfax said there hadn't been such a freeze since his great granny was a girl.

People from all over Kalderdale wrapped up in thick coats, woolly hats and scarves (apart from the youngsters, who disdained such coddling and were in shirtsleeves) and converged on the lake to enjoy sledging, curling, skating, and skittles.

Enterprising hawkers arrived selling chip butties and battered fish with mushy peas. Boatmen, temporarily out of a job, threw up makeshift tents of sailcloth propped up with oars, and sold strong brown ale and even stronger, bowner, tea.

The crowds didn't leave as night drew on. Instead, torches were lit round the lake and people carried lanterns on sticks. There was a brass band, clog dancing, and stalls selling corned beef hash.

There was parkin, fat rascals, slabs of fruit cake served with cheese, and cocoa.

But when the stars pricked patterns in the sky, the merry-making was interrupted by the clarion call of trumpets and the baying of hounds. The crowds lifted awestruck faces to the mountains, and saw the chariots of the gods racing across the sky. And they let out an almighty cheer.

The gods sped on to the Barrel Tops, accompanied by a howling wind from the north carrying flakes of snow. Bretth's falcon spiralled higher and faster, until his wings stirred the air into a spinning tornado. It ripped through the Withies, tearing down the bandits' tents and scattering the contents. Braziers were blown over, throwing out burning wood and ash.

And then a creature from nightmares blotted out the stars. It descended, belching out fire, and its wings crushed the trees. Suffocating smoke blinded the raiders and closed up their throats. Any who stopped to gather up booty found their escape route blocked by flames. The fire spread, devouring the bandits' hide-out. The firedrake swooped low, picking up men and women in its claws and dropping them in the Blackwater, whose waters rose to flood the camp until no trace of it was left.

A man carrying two little girls cried out a plea to the gods. A flash of lightning revealed a track through the trees. He stumbled towards it, and as

218

he and the children escaped, the trees spread out their branches and twined about each other to block the entrance.

Fleeing figures who reached the outskirts of the forest thought they were safe, until they found their ankles entangled by tugging roots. White tubers sprang up and wrapped themselves tightly round their legs, and slithered about their bodies to pin their arms. Slowly, inexorably, they were dragged down into the earth, and the soil closed over their heads.

The gods stormed across the sky. Volte whirled his hammer round his head and thunder rolled under the chariot wheels. The gods hallooed and clashed their weapons, and lighting flashed in answer.

Townsfolk looked up to see The Wild Hunt chasing through the clouds, phantom hounds at their heels, a firedrake wheeling overhead, and closed the shutters with trembling hands, and hid under the blankets.

Oculus, a firebolt clamped in his teeth, roared, 'I love it when a plan comes together!'

***

The cottage in Treegarth was shaken by the passing of the gods. The window frames rattled and hail hammered the glass, threatening to crack it. Leaves blew in from the gap under the door as Dogpole and Vallora knelt over Mopper.

Nothing they did woke her, and Vallora was at her wits' end. She grabbed Dogpole's arm and shouted against the thunder outside.

'We must get her out! It's this place! I knew it was bad from the start! We've got to get her out of here!'

'Have you lost your mind? There's all hell breakin' loose out there!'

'It's the Shydd! He's done something to her, like the Shydd did to Harry! The way she looked at us —I don't think she knows who we are any more. I smelled the Shydd in here as soon as I stepped inside! It's making her ill!'

Her fear and his own antipathy to the Shydd half convinced him. And when the folds of the quilt fell back to reveal the pendant on Mopper's breast, he gasped. Vallora cried out in horror. Dogpole ripped the ribbon of leather and pitched the stone into the hearth. He gathered Mopper into his arms, and he and Vallora ran from the cottage.

They were at the centre of a maelstrom. The sky crackled and fizzed. The oaks surrounding the cottage had split, broken by Sessile's raging boar, which had tossed them on its tusks as if they were sticks of barley sugar.

Icy rain cut Vallora's skin. She put out an arm to

220

protect herself. She was buffeted by a violent gust of wind which lifted her off her feet and slammed her against a tree.

Yards away, Dogpole lay unconscious, Mopper sprawled on top of him. A branch ripped from a tree had knocked him out mid-stride, leaving a gash across his forehead.

Vallora, her hair whipping about her face, called out above the screaming gale. 'Dogpole?' She pushed herself away from the tree. A flash of lightning seared itself across her eyes, and she was thrown sideways into oblivion.

There was sudden silence as if the hurricane had paused to take a shuddering breath. The landscape froze. Whirling leaves hung suspended in the air. Moonlight broke through the clouds...

...'Which one?' The goddess held back the stags, who jostled and shook their antlers, impatient to rejoin the chase.

The shaft of light illuminated three bodies lying unconscious inside a circle of battered trees. Moonbeams brushed the face of one of them like a blessing. Lorelai, leaning from her chariot, exclaimed, 'That one looks familiar! One of yours?'

She was looking down at a young woman of statuesque proportions and glacial beauty, with hair the colour of the night sky.

'Which one do you want?' repeated Umbra icily.

'Oh, the other, of course.'

Umbra lifted her hand. One of the bodies stirred and rose, floating up through the still landscape until its golden head came to rest in Lorelai's arms.

'I can be generous too, but you owe me for this!' said Umbra.

'I owe you nothing! You are merely helping me to right a wrong!'

'*Merely*? There's nothing *mere* about it! Oculus isn't going to like this one bit.' Umbra gathered the silver traces, and the stags leaped into the air.

The goddesses sped away. There was a clap of thunder like the slam of a dungeon door, and the light abruptly disappeared. The storm veered away, resuming its devastating passage across Seywarde.

And Mopper lay in the lap of the gods. Literally.

\*\*\*

When Vallora and Dogpole dragged themselves to their feet, a thick fog hung over the Greenwood. They were soaked with rain, and there was no sign of Mopper. Vallora imagined her wandering alone in the bleak dawn, dazed and ill, looking for them. Or did she even remember them? Her vacant look in the cottage had chilled her heart.

They searched all day until twilight fell and Vallora could see little but the darker shadows of fallen trees. Tired and dispirited, she made her way back to Treegarth and the cottage, and collapsed onto the doorstep.

She didn't know how many hours passed before she was roused by Dogpole' voice. She must have fallen asleep, for she was stiff and cold, and a pale light was breaking in the sky. Dogpole was drawn and grey, and frowned when he saw Vallora was alone.

'Well?' she asked. She sneezed and shivered.

'I looked everywhere. There's no sign of her.'

He eased himself down next to her and wiped a hand across his forehead. They sat silently, too depressed to talk.

After a while Dogpole said, 'You're frozen. You shouldn't have stayed out here.'

'I couldn't go into the cottage again. I can't help thinking—Oh Dogpole!'

His hand was smeared with blood. He wiped it off on his britches. Tears sprang to her eyes at the sight of the deep wound on his forehead.

'Come inside.'

'I don't think I can. Give me a hand.'

He got up stiffly and grimaced as she helped him into the cottage. Her unease about the place was put aside in light of this new worry. She felt guilty for not attending to his wound sooner. She'd neglected it in her haste to look for Mopper. She thought she should have known better than to leave a cut open to infection.

She sat him down and searched for clean cloths, her fingers numb and clumsy. Dogpole gritted his teeth as she dabbed the blood away. The gash was ragged, and when she looked closely she saw there were tiny pieces of bark inside. She hesitated to probe at the wound, fearing she might cause more damage. She found a towel and bound up his head as best she could.

By the time she'd got a fire going, the morning had advanced. She made scrambled eggs, but Dogpole was too exhausted to eat. He slumped in the armchair, and there were beads of perspiration under the improvised bandage. He didn't object when she stripped off his wet clothes and wrapped a blanket round him.

'I've been thinking,' she said. 'Agatta's camp isn't so very far. I think it's likely her people will have found Kat, don't you?'

Dogpole didn't reply.

'They'll be out and about, now the storm's moved on,' she said.

He shifted the chair nearer the fire.

She said, 'Things will be brighter in the morning.' She bit her lip. Her words sounded hollow.

Dogpole's chin dropped to his chest. She put the last log on the fire and carried a chair from the table to sit and watch over him.

***

'What the hell!' Dogpole woke with a start, disturbed by a noise at the door. The towel round his head slipped down over one eye.

Someone was raising the latch. The door swung open and a man stood there, carrying a saddlebag. Behind him, a bay horse stepped delicately through the ruin of Treegarth and sniffed the litter of leaves and branches, his reins trailing.

Dogpole scrabbled around for his machete, but discovered that under the blanket he wore nothing but his breeks. Vallora had hung his wet garments on a clothes horse to dry, and stuffed his wet boots with paper.

Harry came in and dumped the saddlebag onto the table. He glanced at Dogpole, took a knife from his own belt and tossed it across to him, and then leaned against the table, arms folded, watching him coolly.

Dogpole bungled the catch. The blanket fell off. He yanked off the towel, and stood, almost naked, staring at Harry indignantly.

'What the hell?'

'Yes, you said. You swear like a trooper.'

'I swear like a footsoldier, pal. We're the ones with dirty boots.'

'Well, here's your muddy boots, and the rest.' Harry tossed over Dogpole's dry clothes. 'Vallora said to keep an eye on you. She says you need something for your head. She's right. You can't hold a knife, let alone use one.'

He picked up his blade and sheathed it, and then turned his back on Dogpole to unpack the bag. Dogpole struggled into his clothes and looked for his belt.

Vallora came downstairs carrying a bottle, a box of pots, and bandages.

'Oh Dogpole, you're up!' Her eyes were red from lack of sleep. She blinked back tears of relief. 'I was beginning to think you'd never…I want to look at your forehead.'

'What's *he* doin' here?'

'In a minute. That cut's been left too long.' She saw the tension between them. 'Harry, have you been aggravating him when you can see he's not well? Do something useful, will you? See if you can find some scissors, and bring in some logs for the fire. Don't glower at me, Dogpole! Sit down, please. This might sting a bit.'

She held his head still and dripped the contents of the bottle into the wound. He yelped and grabbed her wrist.

'What are you doin' to me? It hurts like hell!'

'It's only an antiseptic. I want to use all of it.'

'That's enough! Tell me what's goin' on!'

Vallora had been right in thinking that Agatta would send out scouts once the tempest had subsided. Most stayed in the camp to clear the debris, but she hadn't forgotten their friends in Fallowdale. She'd sent some men and women to see how far the devastation had spread. Amongst them was Tyler, anxious about his family. He found them safe and well, the children excited about the fire they'd seen in the sky and the strange clouds like monstrous winged beasts.

Harry had ridden out from Withy Woods on the same mission. He knew the farmers, and lent them a hand when barns needed repair or crops needed picking, in return for supplies. At Treorchy Farm he'd joined in helping to patch the broken fencing. He overheard a man talking about three travellers, wondering how they'd fared. Harry questioned him, and soon after he packed up some provisions, and by late afternoon his horse had picked his way through the forest to the cottage.

'He said his name was Tyler and he'd seen you. He was cagey, and took some convincing that I knew you. But in the end he told me where you'd been headed. I hoped you'd still be here, laid up by the storm, and would be glad of some fresh food.'

'We are, thanks. Have you found some scissors?'

He watched Vallora spread salve over Dogpole's forehead. 'Look, I don't mean to pry, but when Tyler told me he'd seen you a couple of days ago, I was surprised. I thought you'd be long gone, back in Diamare with the boy you were looking for. Did you find him? The girl who was with you…?'

'We got separated. Blaise wasn't here.'

Vallora concentrated on securing a pad over the wound, winding a bandage round Dogpole's head to maintain the pressure. She cut the surplus

227

length down the middle, and wrapped the two strips in opposite directions to hold the bandage in place, knotting the ends together and snipping them off. She handed the scissors back to Harry and stood considering him, hands on hips. She thought he deserved more than her terse explanation of events.

Dogpole remained sullenly silent while she described what had happened since they'd left the Bone Cave: the re-appearance of Small Radiance in the Fens, the underground river tunnel, the Shydd's disappearance when they reached the Greenwood, and their encounter with Agatta and her people.

Harry said, 'I'd heard there was a holy woman in the wood. Tyler didn't say anything about a camp.'

'No, he wouldn't,' said Dogpole.

'What's that supposed to mean?'

'I got to spell it out? He didn't trust you, pal! Nor do I!'

'Dogpole!' But Vallora's protest was half-hearted.

'It's the truth! He turns up out of the blue and you welcome him with open arms an' tell him everythin'! What's he told us about what *he* knows? What did the Shydd do to him, and what did that vermin do to Kat? He's known all along, and he's not tellin' us!'

Dogpole, his sickly pallor overlaid by a flush of anger, advanced shakily on Harry. Vallora looked from one to the other, confused.

Harry's lip curled. 'If you're spoiling for a fight I'll be happy to oblige, but I'm not your enemy.'

'We know who is!'

'The Aelythir? There really *is* something wrong with your head!'

'And you're in league with 'em!'

'You're a fool!'

Harry was at the door when Vallora said, 'Help us understand, then. Don't walk away. We haven't found Kat. Do you know what it's like to lose someone?'

His face drained of colour and he looked as if he might strike her, but she stood her ground and stared at him. He hadn't forgotten everything. It wasn't so easy to wipe away your past, after all.

She said, 'It makes you desperate and a bit crazy. I've gone crazy myself, convinced myself of all sorts of nightmares. I don't know what to believe any more.'

He took a breath and slowly unclenched his fist.

'An Aelythir saved my life,' he said shortly. 'I told you that. I was raving like a madman. I could have snapped him in two with my bare hands.'

But Dogpole's jaw was set. 'Maybe so, but Kat got ill after Twinkle—'

'*Twinkle*? Good gods!' muttered Harry.

'...and she couldn't get rid of him! He was a parasite, an encroachin' little—'

Vallora put a hand on his arm. 'You're working yourself up! You'll make yourself worse.' She turned to Harry. 'It was me. I didn't trust him. He said Kat was bound to him, and you were bound to his lord. It frightened me. What did he mean?'

***

Blaise led a charmed life. However he was thrown, he landed on his feet. He was impervious to misfortune, whether it came in the form of conmen, footpads, or bored teenagers in search of excitement. Ill-luck slid off him and couldn't get a grip. Danger dogged his steps, but when it had the opportunity to bite him, it jumped up and licked his face instead, and then rolled onto its back and asked him to tickle its tummy.

And in the hidden realm of the Aelythir he was brought face to face with their prince. Alfyndur's skin was smooth, untroubled by time. But Blaise looked on those composed features, and saw that beneath them the prince's heart was ravaged by hurt and grief.

'My grandfather grieves, too,' said Blaise. 'He misses you. He always has. You must know that.'

And Alfyndur, bereft, was bathed in a sympathy which understood and did not censure. He saw that by punishing his brother he had inflicted wounds on himself. Had he been human, he might have wept for the lost years. And he saw that the boy in front of him was protected by a divine hand. He had no wish to provoke another god.

His reconciliation with Meredydd, despite the influence of Blaise and the perseverance of Olwyn, could only be tentative after so many years of acrimony. In the way of the Aelythir, it was restrained and undemonstrative. And there was little time to devote to it; the Withies was no longer a haven. Umbra, angry with Alfyndur, had left them exposed. In haste, the prince commanded that Lithwyn's broken body be laid in a safe place, deep and dark, and the Aelythir wove charms of protection about him as they prepared to leave Withy Woods.

***

Sunshine prickled against her skin and she wanted to open her eyes, but the light pressed too brightly on her lids. She sank back into cradling arms. On the edge of consciousness, she floated amongst fragmentary sensations. Soaring pillars the colour of sunrise in a sky like a field of cornflowers. A room with the velvety fragrance of roses on a hot summer's day. Voices like a carillon of bells...

'You have freed her from the darkness that bound her. You can't keep her any longer.'

'She's so sweet. She reminds me of me.'

'She won't be sweet if she wakes up here, she'll go mad. They're fragile like that. Remember Hatchu?'

'I won't let her wake up!'

'Then she'll die. You can't keep her.'

The goddess clasped the small form to her breast and gave an aching sigh which would have melted any human heart. 'But I love her!'

'I know. It's very touching and you make a pretty picture. Now put her back where you found her.'

'I can't. You trampled it,' said Lorelai peevishly.

Oculus saw himself leading The Wild Hunt as it tore across the Greenwood bringing ruin.

'Put her somewhere else, then.'

'Where? What haven't you trampled?'

Umbra appeared at the door. She was enveloped in dark robes and a veil protected her from the brightness of the room. She took in the scene.

'How cosy.'

But Oculus would not be deflected. 'I'm not happy about this! It will feed stories we pick up mortals willy nilly and dump them in the Netherworld!'

Umbra bowed her head. Her hair pulled free from its net and cascaded about her shoulders. 'Lorelai is blameless. It is entirely my fault. Let me make amends. I will return the mortal to a place untouched by…by your mighty rout.'

'Alive? Unharmed by this meddling?'

'Unharmed, and with Lorelai's gracious consent, gifted with blessings. Will that satisfy you both?'

Lorelai, pleased to be absolved of blame, was soothed by Umbra's humble words. She agreed, but her lips drooped sadly when the goddess lifted the girl into her own arms.

Oculus was not immune to his wife's plea, or that waterfall of dark hair, but, suspicious, tried to penetrate the folds of Umbra's veil. 'You know I don't like dabbling. You're not going to interfere again, are you?'

'How could I, when I'm sure you would never do so yourself!'

She swept out, leaving Oculus with nothing to say.

\*\*\*

Dogpole felt some strength returning after eating the food Harry had brought. He was grateful, although it came at the cost of listening to Harry hold forth for what seemed to him a tediously long time.

'The Aelythir once believed that if they chose to heal a mortal, they were responsible for that life afterwards. That's what Lithwyn meant by the bond, and why he followed Kat. But there was friendship between them from the first. You must have seen that for yourself.'

Vallora shook her head. She looked doubtfully at Harry's haggard face. 'Are you as close to this lord Alfyndur? Does he protect you?'

Harry said briefly, 'He nursed me through the worst. The  reevers' attacks put a stop to it.'

Vallora thought she understood the reason for his gaunt appearance. Alfyndur had abandoned him. He'd been left only partially free of the poison in his veins, still in pain, and plagued by who knew what nightmares.

Harry saw her appalled expression. 'It wasn't Alfyndur who poisoned me, and I don't blame him for turning against me. His people were being murdered by men like me. He couldn't look at me without revulsion.'

Dogpole broke in on their conversation. He'd fished the pendant from the hearth, and thrust it under Harry's nose.

'This belonged to the Shydd. Kat wore it and—'

Harry was irritated by the interruption. 'You can see it's as easily broken as they are! Did you really believe the little Aelythir could best you?'

'I'm damn sure he couldn't! Not without this!'

'It doesn't make them invincible! There wouldn't be so few of them if it did!' Harry stopped, annoyed with himself for letting Dogpole rile him. He turned to Vallora. 'I don't know anything about the runestone they wear. If it's more than a good luck charm, Alfyndur never told me. But I *do* know the reevers hunt them for sport. That's why the prince turned his back on me. On all mortals.'

Vallora said, 'The Aelythir who helped Kat didn't.'

'Alfyndur will punish him for it.'

'And Kat?'

'When I left, Alfyndur was angry. He said "You take and give nothing back." He blames a mortal for taking his brother away. He said such relationships made his people weak, open to manipulation.'

Vallora snatched up her coat. 'We must find Kat before he does. Will you help, Harry?' Her hands shook as she fumbled with the buttons.

Dogpole said quietly, 'There was no sign of her.'

'Yes, but the storm's over now and it's still light. It'll be easier to get around.' She tipped the contents of the medicine chest into her bag. 'We've got to go.'

Dogpole took her shoulders in a firm grip.

'You're panickin'. Listen to me for once. Kat isn't here. If she'd been in the Greenwood, I'd have found her.'

She stared at him until the full significance of his words hit her. She caught her breath on a sob, and gave him a clumsy embrace. 'Oh Dogpole!'

She knew no-one better at picking up a trail. And he would have pushed himself until he was certain there was no trace of Mopper in the Greenwood. He'd searched the forest, over how many miles and for how many exhausting hours? She'd fallen asleep waiting for him. He'd returned bone-weary, and she hadn't understood when he'd tried to tell her.

'Oh Dogpole!'

'Good gods!' He pulled her from his damp shoulder. 'I know you're tired, we're both tired, but every time you say my name lately you blub. Do you know how that makes me feel? Because it's damn depressin'. No more 'Oh Dogpoles', okay?'

Vallora took a deep breath. After a moment she nodded and straightened her shoulders.

'All right. Kat isn't here. But people don't vanish. She must have gone *some*where.' She thought about what Harry had said about the close bond between Mopper and Small Radiance, and was suddenly alarmed. 'She's gone to rescue the Shydd, hasn't she?'

Harry had listened to them feeling like an outsider, but now he cleared his throat, worried at the direction their discussion was heading.

'If she's gone in search of him, I wouldn't advise you to follow. Alfyndur is absolute lord of those realms and has good reason to hate us. Even the gods do not challenge his authority there.'

Dogpole was exasperated watching Vallora hang on Harry's every word. When had she ever listened to *him* with such attention? It wasn't as if Harry had anything to offer but doom and gloom. But he didn't know Vallora as well as Dogpole did.

'That a fact? You're so smart you know what the gods think? Only, Vallora's already made up her mind, an' I go along with her, because I'm a fool, as you're fond of tellin' me. So you'll take us to this Alfyndur, wherever the hell he is.'

'Did you hear what I said? He will destroy you!'

'I've done nothin' but hear what you got to say.

236

But it comes down to this. Show us the way an' take your chances with the twisted little prince. He don't like you? I don't like you either, an' I'm right here. Your choice.'

***

Cold water sang on her tongue and ran through her body like liquid crystal. She lifted her head from the spring and looked about. The place she'd woken in felt familiar, but she knew she hadn't been there before, and didn't know how she'd got there. She was seeing everything in such sharp focus, her senses so heightened, it made her dizzy. She felt as if her nerve ends were exposed.

She climbed the valley side, her feet sensitive to every change in the ground, intoxicated by the sweet, fresh smell of vegetation, driven by the conviction that Lithwyn was alive and needed her. Where that certainty came from she didn't know.

In front of a cave mouth was a grassy terrace. There was an arch of hawthorn trees, the tracery of their branches glistening with frost. She was shaken by the beauty of her surroundings. She put out a hand to one of the trunks for support, and then snatched it back with a cry. The tree had quivered at her touch as if it recognised her.

At the cave entrance, she faltered.

'They say no-one walks willingly into the realm of the Fair Folk,' she said aloud.

Inside her head, she heard Vallora say, *'I'm not going to turn my back when he's in trouble. Are you?'*

There were passageways like burrows dimly lit by shafts overhead. They ran in all directions so that the Aelythir could emerge when it was safe, and disappear when they felt threatened. It was like an underground version of The Stews, but this place wasn't teeming with energy and colour. The Aelythir had withdrawn into a prison. The air was heavy with an overwhelming sense of loss.

She remembered the little girls in the woods and Vallora's folded arms. *'We can't leave them here.'*

Some instinct drew her to a sloping passage. The roof dipped and the tunnel narrowed, stretching into darkness. The moist, sharp smell of earth was in her nostrils. Halfway along, she had to crawl on hands and knees, then on her elbows, and finally lying flat, digging her fingers into the soil to drag herself forward. And then she couldn't go any further. The way was blocked by a dense thicket of briars which closed off the space between ground and roof.

She knew that beyond the thorny barricade was the cell she had seen in her dream, with Lithwyn enclosed by curling tree roots. But the paralysing atmosphere of defeat sapped her strength. Her sigh echoed back to her along the empty passage. You will fail. You're not up to it. You let down your friends.

*'Come on, Kat! You're a match for anythin' you'll*

*find in the Withies!'*

She raised her head and took a ragged breath, and began pulling at the brambles. Tears scalded her cheeks as the thorns tore at her skin. Pain rang in her head. She kept stubbornly on. Her arms and hands were bleeding and raw, and after a while, numb. Twigs clawed at her face and tugged at her hair…

The cloud of pain thickened and brought her to a standstill, so that she gasped and covered her ears. There was a noise in her head unconnected to the complaints of her sore body. She tried to quieten her thumping heart and force herself to breathe slowly.

Into her mind came the image of Lithwyn in the Greenwood, his hand on the bark of an oak, his ear pressed to it, listening. Watching him, she, too, had felt at one with the forest. The hawthorn at the entrance to Alfyndur's kingdom had responded to her touch. It was sentient.

She shut her eyes. Tentatively, she reached out to the briars. And was at once rocked back on her heels by a noise of anger and hurt in her head. And behind it she sensed their need to protect. The stems under her fingers trembled, alert to her. She grasped them firmly and tried to communicate her own resolve. The barbs dug into her flesh but she held on, while blood dripped from her fingers and palms and ran down her arms. She saw it seep into the soil and imagined the network of fibrous

239

roots underground. They spread out, connecting the trees and plants, sharing not only nutrients, but knowledge.

She thought she must have fainted and fallen, but the briars had suddenly given way, and she was inside the cell where the Aelythir had laid Lithwyn. Shoots pushed through the soil, the tendrils bending over his broken body in gentle embrace. She reached in to lift him, and carried him through the tunnels to the surface.

The moon was a pale ghost overhead. A group of Aelythir huddled under the trees. They shrank away when she approached, and would not meet her eyes. She recognised the prince with the copper circlet, but he seemed crushed, no longer the imperious figure who had emerged from the mist to confront her. He was leaning for support on two others, a slender woman and a man very like him, with a face marked by sorrow.

She faced the prince and spoke in a voice which was not entirely her own.

*'I know he is alive. Remorse has blinded you. It is a human emotion and achieves nothing. But you are not mortal. You are Lord of the Aelythir. Look after your own.'*

His eyes blazed at her words but he was more unsettled by what he saw. A girl stood in front of him, against whom he'd poured his resentment for all the ill-treatment inflicted on the Aelythir by mortals. She held on to Lithwyn, though she was torn and bleeding, and shook with the effort. He had said *'You take and give nothing back'* and this girl confused and challenged him.

She confronted him, certain that the limp body of Lithwyn held a spark of life, and that Alfyndur could heal him. The prince rubbed a hand across his eyes, unsure of himself. The goddess had turned her back on him. He felt powerless, as broken as the body the girl carried.

His brother stepped forward to take Lithwyn and lay him on the grass. The girl staggered and sank to her knees. Alfyndur turned his golden eyes on her and she felt as if he looked into her heart.

She held her breath when he knelt by Lithwyn.

He closed his eyes and his lips moved as he said some words. Lithwyn lay unmoving. Alfyndur's skin became grey with effort, but still Lithwyn did not stir. Alfyndur bowed his head in defeat.

He felt his brother's steadying grip on his shoulder. After a moment, the prince put his hand on Lithwyn's brow. All at once brilliant white light spilled from his fingers…

…When Mopper came to, she was lying on grass in a cold dawn, and Lithwyn was getting to his feet. Where Alfyndur's fingers had touched his forehead, marks like the points of a star were burned into his skin. Lithwyn put a hand to his breast and smiled at her.

*'We go to our people in the haven you call Shydding.*

*Fare well, beloved of the goddess.'*

The young woman who'd supported Alfyndur ran forward and clung to the prince's brother. Gently, he unclasped her arms from his neck. The prince's hand rested fleetingly on her head, and then, leaning on his brother, he walked away.

Mopper held her hand against a sudden burst of sunshine as a figure came through the trees. Through her tears she saw a warrior in a golden helmet wielding a sword. She shook her befuddled head. When she was able to focus, she saw it was a boy with bright hair carrying a walking staff.

'Blaise?'

'We're going home, but we'll see you to Diamare first.' Blaise gave his radiant, sympathetic smile. 'Don't worry. It'll be all right.'

***

The Withies was a very different place. Where once it had been clogged with close-packed, thin trees, lightning had struck the forest and fire had cleared open spaces. They clambered over charred wood, through burned, stunted trees and smouldering ash. The air was heavy with acrid smoke, but in places daylight had begun to pierce the wood's murky secrets, promising an end to its long hibernation.

They came to an area of the forest untouched by The Wild Hunt and Harry slowed, looking about him. Here the trees glowed in shades of orange and red, echoing the fire. The ground began folding into a series of valleys. Harry stopped when they reached a glade whose slopes were covered in hazel, and holly bright with clusters of berries. Vallora and Dogpole followed him, clambering over blocks of crumbling masonry, past tumbled walls and broken columns. In the centre, a cairn of white pebbles had been placed around a spring. It splashed down onto a stone, and had carved out a hollow filled with clear, icy water.

Harry pointed to the opposite slope, where a cliff face rose from a terrace. When they'd climbed to the top, he said, 'Alfyndur made it clear a long time ago that I was no longer welcome. It won't help you if he sees my face.'

Dogpole glowered but Vallora said, 'Thank you for bringing us this far.'

He looked at their set expressions, then nodded,

and went swiftly back down the slope.

Vallora and Dogpole strode together through a whitethorn hedge onto a stretch of grass. Groups of trees stood like sentinels guarding an opening in the rock. Briars grew round it. A few wild flowers hung on, their petals washed of colour, shrivelling in the crisp air.

Past the cave mouth was a maze of tunnels, and they tensed at every turn, expecting to be challenged. They discovered the dwelling-places of the Aelythir, like cells in a honeycomb. They found the gloomy hall of the prince's audience chamber, and deeper still, his dungeon. The air carried the musky smell of the Aelythir, but there was no sign of them, nor of Mopper.

Dogpole, deprived of action, hit his fists against the silent walls in frustration. He reeled away from the cave and gasped in cold breaths of air, striving for control.

Vallora followed him out, and dropped to the grass. The adrenalin which had sustained her had drained away. Dogpole saw that the dark smudges under her eyes were more pronounced. Anxiety and fatigue had etched creases around her mouth. She was running on empty.

He said, 'I'm goin' to have a look around but I need to concentrate. The ground is hard. Frost. An' it's gettin' dark. It's not goin' to help if you're fidgetin' about, firin' questions at me I can't answer.'

She nodded dumbly. She expected that he'd bound into action but he simply stood and did nothing at all. She hadn't the energy to quiz him, and she'd promised to be quiet. She held herself still and watched.

Dogpole remained passive, taking in the area. He was looking for anything which seemed out of place. After a few minutes, he took off his heavy coat, folded it, and placed it out of the way, near Vallora. He stepped over to an area beyond the cave mouth and knelt down.

There was a shallow dip in the ground. Changes in the colour of the soil showed where it had been disturbed—within the last twelve hours, or the moisture in the darker patch would have evaporated. Further on, a foot had kicked up speckles of earth onto a clump of weed. Nearer to the trees, flattened stalks of grass shone white where they had been crushed. They pointed to the direction the boots had taken. He moved towards the trees, his steps painstakingly slow and deliberate. Vegetation had been bruised by the passage of feet. A broken twig at shoulder height twisted in the air, hanging from a single white fibre.

The sky darkened and it got colder. Vallora rubbed her stiff limbs. Dogpole was some distance away, stooping to examine the ground beyond the trees. His discarded coat was close by. She dragged it towards her, and lay underneath the fur,

245

patiently watching his plodding figure, her head pillowed on one arm.

Dogpole waited until he heard the regular rhythm of her snores. Then he straightened and fumbled about for his cigarettes. He lit one and stared up into the night sky. The new moon was low, peering at him curiously.

It had taken him only minutes to establish that two groups had left, in different directions. The larger group, lightly-built and barefoot, left few signs on the frozen ground. He traced them going east, hugging the trees and the curve of the river.

He was more interested in the second group, who had headed straight for the West March Road. There were three, each with a distinct footprint. One hardly disturbed the grass. The others wore boots. The first took long, confident strides. The span suggested someone tall, and from the depth of the indents, heavily-built. The other's steps were shorter and left a fainter impression. He scrutinised the lighter prints with particular intensity.

Dogpole drew on his cigarette. Vallora still lay in a sleep of utter exhaustion. The cold must have made him light-headed, because he looked up at the eye of the moon and grinned.

*\*\**

Olwyn hoped that in time Blaise might be the means of reconciling Aelythir and mortals. But first there was the matter of a reconciliation closer to home.

She clung to Blaise as they walked up the drive. The doors of the house stood open. People were gathered on the steps. A girl ran to fling herself into Blaise's arms.

Olwyn recognised the steward and the housekeeper. She guessed the flame-haired young woman was the mistress of Old Hall. She was beaming at Debs' tearful welcome of Blaise. But Orson's eyes were locked on Olwyn's face with that familiar, slightly anxious expression, as if he half expected her to vanish when he blinked.

Everyone came down the steps to greet Blaise. Mistress Jessup reached up to hug him and patted him, to be sure it was really him, safe and sound. He stood, a little abashed, while the housekeeper tried to extricate him from the well-wishers and take him inside.

Orson stood apart, the same shaggy bear of a man Olwyn remembered, but thicker round the waist, and with grey hairs amongst the red. Seeing him with Blaise, she thought the resemblance so striking she was surprised he didn't see it at once.

'Welcome to Old Hall,' said Lord Natchbold stiffly. 'You and...'

'Our son,' said Olwyn.

The inhabitants of Seywarde counted the cost of the wreckage left by The Wild Hunt.

In his mountain fastness, Don Alejandro was told by a nervous steward that he had lost a third of the trees from his parkland. The tempest had also torn down the cramped tenements and shoddily-built dwellings which had sprung up on the eastern edge of his estate. From the battlements of Wulfshaven he glimpsed the pristine whiteness of the frozen park, and regretted the absence of some familiar stands of trees. He could just make out the miserable exodus of refugees trudging away from the flattened shacks. Their tracks would soon be covered by the falling snow. They were making for the solid walls of an empty building which had once been the Temple of the Brothers of Boundaries. He thought that, on the whole, the gods had been even-handed.

In Diamare, sober worthies patrolled the streets, noting which buildings had suffered most. This far south, little remained of the previous night's snowfall. The gutters ran with brown meltwater.

The Mayor was relieved to find that the citizens had sustained only minor injuries. The force of the storm had been directed at the temples, which in the small hours were deserted. A group of children scrambled about the ruins of one, gleefully seeking out the last pockets of snow to squeeze into balls.

The snowman they'd built was already melting, a grotesque figure with a pin-head and one eye, its twig arms in the slush.

The Stews were unscathed. The Mayor thought that if anything would have benefited from a good scathing it was those pestilential streets. But even the winds of The Wild Hunt could not penentrate the thick fug of its alleyways. No doubt Dave Hamm's scrapyard business would profit from the clearing-up process. But there were also buildings to repair, and the Mayor had friends in the trade, so it wasn't all bad news.

In the countryside, forests had been ravaged by fire. Ice had frozen rivers in the north, and torrential rain had flooded their banks in the west. But the crops were already harvested, safely stored in barns which remained miraculously untouched, and there was only stubble in the fields when wind swept Midgarden's plains and buffeted Southron's orchards. The farmers grumbled, but farmers always grumble. Everyone agreed it could have been worse.

For a week, people were agog with a story that the gods had plucked up a poacher from the Greenwood and forced him to join The Wild Hunt. Or it was a shepherdess who was taken up. Or a sheep. The rumour was soon discounted, because countryfolk are a superstitious lot, and you can't believe a thing they say.

Of real concern was the assault on the temples.

There was no escaping that they'd been the prime target of the gods' wrath. The priests and priestesses of Seywarde had to confront the fact that the Pantheon wasn't happy with the way they were running things. The temples sent their bigwigs to a Convocation in Summerston. Because when bigwigs gather for important meetings, they choose a town with comfortable hotels, where there is a good choice of restaurants, shops and cultural amenities to enjoy during the downtime.

The Hi-Hatt from The Little Sisters of Justice in Piersport, where Lorelai's shrine lay shattered, warned of further destruction, something she called Divine Retribution, if they didn't change their ways. Anemone Marlin, from the temple of the water goddess in Norvik, advised them to avoid tails in statuary. Chaz Lamplighter, the self-styled Fist of Volte from the ruined temple in Dom Rei, said it was an opportunity to clear out dead wood. Like payment for prayers, free breakfasts, and mercenary high priests like Magister Greybody. A cleric who'd fled the destruction of the House of the Winds in Platt Obscura agreed fervently.

And Patroness Hildegard from the Sanctuary of the Marsh said they should return to the precepts Aquaphraya herself had brought to Seywarde. The bigwigs nodded sagely. They couldn't recall precisely what the goddess had said, but when they returned to their temples, they thumbed through ancient scrolls to find her original words.

Before other people had come along and added ideas of their own. They discovered the Pantheon hadn't recommended any of the observances, sanctions, and customs which had grown up since.

When Hildy knelt, straight-backed, to update the gods, she was able to report that the temples had ditched many of the customs which had angered them.

***

Vallora and her friends were on what the newly-appointed captain called 'compassionate leave'. But there had been no compassion in her basilisk eyes when she demanded they gave an account of themselves. The lost spit boy had returned to Old Hall under his own steam. She doubted if he'd been lost at all.

Captain Velvet had been promoted from Dom Rei Guards to replace the disgraced Fletcher. She was a veteran officer, despite her youth. Or perhaps she was not so much youthful as well-preserved. She had eyes like raisins set in a bloodless face, and an arrangement of teeth which made the hairs on Dogpole's neck stand on end.

It was clear she had nothing but contempt for Fletcher. When they told her he'd not only agreed to their search for Blaise, but had ordered them to leave without delay, she gave a withering look.

'Fletcher wanted you out of the way before the

Inspector arrived. He sent you on a wild goose chase and you fell for it. Captain Bell gave me a favourable report of you, but I think he was misled.' She sent Vallora a pointed look.

Mopper stared owlishly at the Captain. She could see that Velvet was pleased to have found a weakness in the admired Captain Bell's judgement.

Captain Velvet tapped her long fingernails on the desk. 'You exploited the situation. You used your positions and the resources of the Guards to go on some sort of personal jolly. I suggest you take a couple of weeks to consider your options.'

'With respect—' began Vallora politely.

'With respect?' Captain Velvet smiled bleakly, and Dogpole shuddered. 'I've heard about your respect for the Guards. And in case you pretend to misunderstand me, let me be clear. I wasn't actually making a suggestion. Two weeks.'

Back in Mopper's room in Peat Street, Dogpole opened a bottle of beer and said, 'What options is she talkin' about?'

'She means we don't have any. She expects us to resign before we're sacked,' said Mopper.

He shrugged. 'Won't be the first time I been sacked.'

'Are you going to explain? Or are you being irritating about your mysterious past, as usual?'

'Just bein' irritatin'.'

Vallora thought they were putting on a show of light-heartedness for her benefit. 'I'm sorry. I got you into this. It's my fault you've lost your jobs.'

Mopper snorted. 'We've got minds of our own. You're always saying 'It's my fault' as if everything revolved round you!'

Vallora flushed.

Dogpole got up restlessly. 'I keep tellin' you, you don't shoulder everythin' yourself. You might give us some credit now an' again.' He helped himself to another beer. 'I won't miss Staple. An' that new captain is a pain in the neck.'

'Very droll,' said Mopper.

'Roddy Blench will be 'eartbroken you're on furlough,' said Dogpole with relish. 'Might do 'imself a mischief. Wiv' any luck.'

They were doing their best to establish a feeling of normality, but they were not entirely at ease with one another, and the banter was forced. When Vallora and Dogpole had returned to Diamare and found Mopper safe, they were so overjoyed and relieved, that was all that had seemed to matter. And then, when they'd had time to digest everything that had happened, they felt estranged.

Dogpole had been thinking about old comrades who didn't need explanations about his past. There was an ease to such uncomplicated relationships he missed.

Vallora was considering the practicalities of their position. Someone has to, she thought. We'll be paid to the end of the  month, and then what? Whatever Dogpole and Mopper say, they've got used to looking to me to make decisions. And I've got used to being in charge. Has it made me as arrogant as they say? I know I don't always make the best call, but, gods! it isn't plain sailing being the captain in charge of a bickering crew!

She smiled to herself. It was an apt image, because she'd been thinking of Mohavia. She wondered if Stefan had his own ship by now. No-one had any expectations of her at home. At best she was ignored. Right now that sounded appealing.

They were both aware of a change in Mopper. She didn't smile so readily, and was quiet, trying to resolve some problem she had so far been unwilling to share with them. And sometimes, when they caught her looking at them, she would turn quickly away as if embarrassed.

Mopper had found herself in the kingdom of the Aelythir convinced Lithwyn was alive and that she had been sent there to save him. She didn't know how she'd got there and didn't understand much of what had happened afterwards. Back in the solidity of Diamare's grimy streets, her story would have sounded like something she'd dreamed up. As unlikely as travelling amongst the stars…

Her experiences had been disturbing and bewildering, and she'd thought, *hoped*, they would end with her return to Peat Street. Instead, she saw everything with the sharp new awareness she'd woken to in the Withies. She sensed the thoughts of people around her. Walking to The Carter's Arms, she was assaulted by the doubts and desires of everyone she passed. Her head rang with voices she didn't want to hear. If this was a gift, it was a gift she didn't want. She didn't know how to control it.

The worst thing was that she didn't know how to avoid hearing the thoughts of Vallora and Dogpole. She tried to block them out by digging her nails into her palms and concentrating on the words they were saying. She felt like an intruder. How could she explain it to her friends?

A discordant noise from the street broke in on her thoughts. Involuntarily she said, 'Someone outside is unhappy.'

'It's those blasted moggies,' said Dogpole. 'They start screechin' as soon as it gets dark and it sets off all the stray dogs.'

He went to the window, opened it, and emptied the contents of his bottle. There was a startled cry from below. He peered down. 'Kat?'

She joined him. A young man stood in the road. He held a mandolin. A sticky substance dripped from the brim of his hat.

He called up to Mopper. 'Hi. It's, um, it's a serenade. To welcome you home.' He indicated the ill-used instrument. 'Haven't quite mastered it.'

Mopper looked down at his stricken face. 'Thank you, Rodney. No-one's ever…serenaded me before.'

She heard stifled laughter behind her.

'Thought I'd give it a go,' said the young man. 'Thought you might like it. Sort of thing girls like.'

'Is it? Well, that's very thoughtful of you.'

There was a barely suppressed guffaw. Mopper turned from the window, blushing, and said crossly, 'Will you two shut up!'

Rodney looked embarrassed. 'I…sorry, I wasn't expecting you to have guests. I'll give it a go another time. Probably need to practise.'

'Actually, there'll be plenty of time to practise, because I'm going away tomorrow. On a holiday. I'm saying goodbye to my friends.'

She hadn't known she was going to say that, but as soon as she did, it made sense. She would go to Shydding Forest. Lithwyn would help her come to terms with abilites that overwhelmed her.

Below, Rodney looked downcast. 'I heard about the compassionate leave. See you when you get back, then.'

'Yes. Goodnight, Rodney.'

\*\*\*

'No-one appreciates the effort and concentration it takes to bring nightfall to Seywarde, with all the seasonal variations…'

'I'm sure they do, my love.'

'I've a good mind to take a holiday, and then everyone would realise…'

256

'No, Evening Star! No more holidays! What is really upsetting you?'

A shadow passed over Umbra's luminous face.

'I had to be very severe with Alfyndur.'

'I thought you showed admirable restraint. I'd have skewered him for impiety.'

'Will he recover, do you think?'

'It depends entirely on him,' said Oculus. 'That's the beauty of free will.'

'Free will?' Umbra glanced at him. With an occasional nudge to the board, she thought.

'Yes, my love,' said Oculus smoothly. He held out a basket. 'I called on the…on my grandmother this morning. That malevolent bag of bones she calls a pet has had kittens. Must be something to do with the magnetic field up there. Granny can't keep them. Grimalkin is jealous.'

But Umbra had stopped listening as soon as she laid eyes on the basket. Inside were two little kittens with fur as soft as dusk. They miaowed piteously as if they were starved—the most abandoned, helpless creatures in the world.

'Oh, you poor darlings!' said Umbra, bewitched.

***

Printed in Poland
by Amazon Fulfillment
Poland Sp. z o.o., Wrocław

65222304R00157